Forget-Me-Nots & Fireworks

Elle Nicoll

Rose Hope Publishing Ltd.

Copyright © 2022 By Elle Nicoll

All rights reserved.

Visit my website at

Cover Design: Sarah at The Book Cover Boutique

Formatting: Atticus

Editing: Heart Full of Reads

No part of this book may be reproduced or transmitted in any form or by any means, electronically or mechanically, including photocopying, recording, or by any information storage and retrieval system without the written permission of the author, except for the use of brief quotations in a book review.

This book is a work of fiction. Names, characters, places, and incidents are either products of the author's imagination or are used fictitiously. Any resemblance to actual persons, living or dead, events, or locales is entirely coincidental.

CW—This book is intended for adult readers only and contains profanities, detailed sexual acts and reference to medical conditions and memory loss.

Contents

		V
1.	Trent	1
2.	Shona	7
3.	Trent	13
4.	Shona	27
5.	Trent	39
6.	Shona	45
7.	Trent	57
8.	Shona	67
9.	Shona	77
10.	Trent	85
11.	Shona	101
12.	Trent	105
13.	Trent	111
14.	Shona	119
15.	Shona	131

16.	Trent	139
	Epilogue	
17.	Elle's Books	142
18.	Wild Blooms	143
19.	Acknowledgments	145
20.	About Elle	147

To everyone that loves a hero who will make the stars fall for you
x

Please turn back to copyright page for content warnings

Chapter 1
Trent

"Hello, you're through to Cygnature Blooms, where bigger is always better. We specialize in healing broken hearts worldwide. May I have your location...um...please...I mean, if that's okay?"

"Cut!"

I hurl my script onto the floor and rise out of my director's chair before coming around to stand in front of the camera screen. The female actor's eyes widen, her gaze skittering around before she looks back at me.

"It's not working," I bark.

"Okay, let's roll again, from the top," my assistant, Jonathan, calls, spinning his hand in the air and motioning to the camera woman.

"No." I wave at the camera, stepping in front of it and onto the set. I say set, but today we're filming in a real florist shop for a scene in *Steel Force*, a US-based FBI action series.

I walk over to the young actor who looks like a deer in headlights as she nervously chews on her bottom lip.

"Take a break, Michaela." I grimace. I will need serious words with casting if this is the caliber of actor they think they can waste my time with.

Everyone comes to Hollywood to chase that dream. To be discovered. Be the next big thing.

Hardly anyone has what it takes.

Michaela scuttles off, and someone comes and stands next to me.

"Nerves?"

I turn and lock eyes with Jay Anderson, the show's lead. This is the man who actually does have what it takes.

"What the hell, Jay?" My shoulders sag as I run a hand over my jaw and exhale a frustrated breath. "It's only a couple of blasted lines. We're going to be here until midnight at this rate."

My eyes dart to the owner of the florist shop, who's sitting looking at his watch. He was enthusiastic about *Steel Force* being filmed here. But now we're running over schedule, I can sense all those Mother's Day orders he has to fill is wearing his patience thin. A lot like mine is after seven takes of the same scene, which will air for a grand total of twenty-one seconds at the beginning of the episode.

"It'll come together." Jay's blue eyes crinkle at the corners in his signature way that sends the world's press wild and has helped turn him into one of Hollywood's most lusted after male actors.

If he wasn't such a decent guy, it'd be so damn easy to hate him.

"Why don't you ask one of the crew to stand in while Michaela looks over the lines again. It's first-time nerves. We all had them." He looks at his costume's bulletproof vest and adjusts one of the Velcro straps.

"Maybe. But if you can't get a grip on them, then no-one's going to hold your hand here. Hollywood isn't a fucking kindergarten," I mutter, making him chuckle.

"Let's move on!" I shout, causing the crew to fall silent.

Michaela might have pulled herself together enough to redeem herself by the time we've finished. Although, I doubt it. She'll join the long line of actors I've seen boarding a Greyhound back to whatever small town they were in when they believed in the Hollywood dream, and naivety actually convinced them they had a shot. This town's happy ever after movies instilling the 'you can have it all if you only wish it hard enough', have a lot to answer for. It's why I prefer working on action series and thriller films.

My specialism is special effects, and my company isn't just the biggest in Hollywood, it's the largest in the world. This special invitation from the *Steel Force* producers to act as director for the current season isn't the one I'd usually take. But I made time because every episode, I get to destroy something. Blow it up. Set fire to it. Crash it. It feeds the warped part of my soul that was created when my fiancée left me for my now ex-best friend and business partner.

Fucking weasels.

"Jay. Just let me... There." One of the crew's resident makeup artists joins us and dusts her oversized brush over Jay's forehead. She steps back, instrument poised in hand, as she narrows her eyes, tipping her head to the side and studying him. "Great! You're good to go." She grins and one of the set lights catches her long dark ponytail, making it shine like moonlight on the surface of a darkened lake.

The lilt in her voice, and the way her eyes light up as she internally assures herself she's done a good job has me staring at her.

As if sensing my eyes on her, she looks at me.

"You're the one," I state.

She glances at Jay, then back at me.

"I—"

"Change of plan!" I bark, raising a hand in the air and effectively grinding the set crew to a halt again. "We run the scene again with..." I look at the dark-haired woman.

"Shona..." she answers.

"...with Shona playing the role of the florist." I bend and swipe my discarded script up from the floor. "You know the lines, right? You've heard them all morning."

"I... I do." She watches me carefully.

"Excellent. Then let's get going. Places!" I yell, turning to stand behind the camera monitor.

"But I'm not an actor."

I look back into her vibrant hazel eyes, copper lacing her pupils like a ring of flames.

"You are now." I point to the spot behind the florist counter. "You're the one I want, Shona. Now please, take your position and let's finally wrap this fucking scene up."

Chapter 2
Shona

"Watch out this morning, ladies. Sparky's on the war path!"

I smile at Ralph as he hands me my coffee, white, no sugar, steaming hot, just how I like it. He beams at me. I swear he's one of the most loved guys on the *Steel Force* set. Not just because he supplies all the cast and crew with our much-needed five a.m. pick-me-ups, but because he's such a sweet guy. He reminds me of my grandfather, always smiling and willing to lend a hand.

"Oh, great. What's he moaning about now?" Gloria—the set's other makeup artist—stops organizing her brushes, her neon pink nails poised over them as she turns her gaze to Ralph.

"Beats me," Ralph chuckles, letting out a wheeze that turns into a cough. "Something about mis-labeled props."

Sparky is the crew's nickname for Trent Forde, a Special Effects genius, and the guest director on this season of the show.

"Surely, a visit from you cheered him up?"

"I'm no magician, ladies." Ralph shrugs as he heads to the door of the trailer.

"Could have fooled us," Gloria chirps as she inclines her paper cup toward Ralph.

She spins to face me as Ralph leaves.

"You haven't had sex in years, Shona. Do us all a favor and bang the bad attitude out of Trent, will you?"

I splutter, then wince, as I swallow a giant mouthful of coffee. It's either that or spit it out. I'd rather burn my throat than risk ruining the thousands of dollars' worth of makeup kit that I'm standing next to.

"What?" I look at Gloria as I grab a tissue and dab at my lips.

She smooths her short blonde hair behind her ear, completely unfazed. It's as though she's said there's a chance of rain today, not suggested I have sex with the giant pain in the ass known as Trent Forde.

"It'll be like hitting two targets with one arrow," she continues. "Stops your waxes going to waste and cheers up Grumpy Guts. Plus, he seems to like you after you filmed that scene last week and saved us from an entire day of re-takes."

I narrow my eyes at her.

"The whole crew will thank you," she singsongs.

"Okay, so, that would be a no." I put my coffee down and gather my hair up into a high ponytail.

I can't think of anything worse. Trent Forde is grumpy, abrasive, and downright rude sometimes.

Being a genius in your field is no excuse for sending young actors crying to their trailers.

Gloria smirks. "Fine. I bet he's a great bang though. Can't work with explosives and exciting shit all day and not know how to fuck like a—"

"Not interrupting, am I? I can come back later."

Jay Anderson steps in through the trailer door, dressed in sweatpants and a white t-shirt. Gloria's eyebrows shoot up her forehead as his six-foot two frame of pure muscle, topped off with devilishly sexy, dirty-blond hair comes in, bringing with it a delicious waft of freshly showered masculinity.

"Not at all," I answer quickly.

He grins at us.

He heard every word.

"You can interrupt me anytime." Gloria winks.

Jay's a good sport, otherwise Gloria's shameless flirting would have gotten her in trouble by now.

My shoulders shake as I hold in my laugh.

"Come, take a seat." I pat the chair in front of the mirror. Jay sits and tosses an amused grin at Gloria.

I set to work, tucking tissue around his collar and blending the right shade of base on the back of my hand.

"You know I'm only letting Shona do you this morning instead of me because she needs cheering up." Gloria looks at Jay pointedly, her arms crossed.

"Is that so?" His eyes rise to meet mine in the mirror as I reach for my blending sponge.

I start work on him, dabbing the sponge beneath his eyes. God, a man this beautiful makes my job easy.

"Ignore her, Jay. I'm fine."

Gloria tuts. "You are not fine." She addresses Jay again, "It's been months since she had her way with a hot man. She's turned all serious on me."

I take a deep breath. "Thank you for sharing that, Gloria."

"Ah, lighten up, Shona. Jay's our friend." She winks at him again.

I catch his eye, and he smiles at me. We both know Gloria's teasing. She would never betray my trust, not really. We've been friends since I lived with my mom and brother, Josh, and we were neighbors. She might joke about my relationship status, or lack of one. But she'd never tell anyone about the frantic phone calls, the bruises, the tears. About the night she called the police after hearing the screams. About how she drove me and Mom to the hospital, never leaving our side as they fixed up the physical damage.

Gloria is the one who helped bandage the other damage, the torn pieces no-one else saw.

"I know what you're thinking." She points a large blending brush at me with a grin. "You're thinking what an amazing friend I am."

"Something like that," I mutter, my lips stretching into a smile as I continue working.

"Don't get used to me sharing, though. I'm having Jay back as soon as we get a hot man to sort you out." Her gaze trails over his broad chest.

"Your inner cougar is well and truly out this morning." I laugh as I lean closer to Jay, inspecting my work. He laughs too. Gloria's old enough to be his mom.

Maybe that's how she gets away with it. Or are older women his thing. What do I know? He's never had a serious girlfriend that he's mentioned.

"She's always out. Insatiable appetite," Gloria hums.

The three of us are still laughing as the trailer door is thrust open with a bang that makes the thin walls shake.

"The kit bags for the helicopter scene. Anyone seen them?"

Trent Forde looms in the doorway like a storm cloud on a wedding day. His shirt sleeves are rolled up, exposing his thick, corded forearms, and his dark hair falls toward his flushed face.

He would be devastatingly handsome if it weren't for his downright ugly attitude.

"Doesn't the props manager have that all organized?" I snap, my hand hovering mid-brush sweep over Jay's face.

Who the hell does he think he is, barging in here like that?

The lights around the dressing table mirror flicker, and I curse, temporarily breaking eye contact with Trent. They've been doing it on and off for a week now. And despite reporting it to maintenance, they haven't been fixed.

Gloria sucks in a breath, barely loud enough for anyone but me to hear. I know what she's thinking—no one answers Trent back. But frankly, this guy gets on my last nerve. He stomps around the set, setting everyone on edge, and dragging the energy down. No wonder his fiancée left him. It's enough to make me want to jump on a rocket and go into orbit to get away from him.

"Well, you'd like to think so," he growls. "But it seems I'm surrounded by idiots today." He spins abruptly, muttering incoherently.

"I guess maintenance can check if the door still has its hinges when they come to fix the mirror," I say.

He pauses in the doorway and glances at the offending mirror as the bulbs flash again.

Then he stomps off, huffing.

"Told you." Gloria smirks. "Did you see that crazed glint in his eyes? Out of this world orgasm giver, that one. You know you want to, Shona."

Jay snickers as I glare at Gloria.

"Yeah, a walking advert for why I'm better off not dating."

"We'll see," Gloria hums as I shake my head with a grumble.

How about we don't.

Chapter 3
Trent

"Fucking ridiculous," I mutter as I wedge the door to the props room open with a box. I spot the kit bags that no-one could find, yet here they are, miraculously over the far side of the room, just where I said they would be.

Too damn late.

We filmed another couple of scenes due to the 'missing' bags. They'll have to wait until tomorrow now.

I rub a hand over my jaw, casting my gaze around until it lands on what I was hoping might be in here.

"You'll work." I reach out a hand, then draw it back suddenly as a loud bang echoes off the walls, sending the un-windowed props room into darkness.

"Don't tell me you just let the fucking door close!" I snap, unable to conceal the disbelief in my voice.

"It's fine, I'll just hit the light. Don't get your panties in a twist," a delicate voice calls back.

"Fuck's sake," I mutter as the lights flick on, glaringly bright and making me squint.

Shona pushes her long, dark hair over one shoulder and then folds her arms across her chest and looks at me.

"Didn't you see the memo that was sent around? The door's been acting up." I stride past her, my step faltering as the scent of something intoxicating and floral fills my nostrils.

I grab the door handle and pull.

Nothing.

"Hey!" I hammer a fist against the thick wood, gritting my teeth. The last member of the stage crew left for the evening as I came in.

Fucking brilliant.

I turn and am met with a cool stare and pursed lips.

"Are you going to answer my question?"

One dark brow arches at me.

"Are you going to stop acting like a jerk?"

"I—"

She stares at me, waiting.

I run a hand around the back of my neck and exhale a long breath.

"I shouldn't have snapped. Apologies," I mutter.

What the hell has gotten into me? Apologizing?

Popularity means little to me. I'd rather people think my work is incredible and my personality is shit, given the choice of one or the other. So why am I suddenly apologizing to this—my eyes drop over her, and I swallow—this *beautiful* woman?

Because she won't take your nonsense and she challenges you, a voice that sounds remarkably like my mother's jests inside my head.

"Apology accepted." Shona takes in the door handle, which I'm still firmly grasping, like it will magically open.

I turn it and rattle the door again, for effect.

"Like the memo said. The door needs fixing. It can only be opened from the outside. That's why I had it propped open."

"Then let's call someone to come and open it."

She looks at me and I'm struck by how mesmerizing her eyes are. That same copper halo around her pupil I first noticed when we were filming on location in the florist shop burns brightly.

A ring of fire.

One side of my mouth lifts. Maybe this is where she gets the fiery personality from.

"Go ahead. Then we can get out of here for the evening."

"My phone's in my coat. Can you call?" she says.

"I don't have mine."

Her eyes widen and her plump bottom lip drops from the perfect cupid's bow on top.

"You're the set director, and you don't have your phone?" She looks at me like I've told her I'm not a special effects artist, but a wizard who learned his magic at Hogwarts while bunking in with HP himself.

"It's charging on my desk. I only came in for one thing. I wasn't planning on getting locked inside the fucking room."

Her brows pull together as she resumes her earlier unimpressed, cool assessment of me.

"And that's my fault?"

"You were the one who closed the door." Heat builds in my chest, but I force a deep breath into my lungs to relax my shoulders. "Never mind."

"Someone will miss us. They're bound to." She walks across the room, her heels clicking on the tiled floor before she perches on the edge of a table loaded with boxes.

"Like your boyfriend, if you're late?"

Her eyes snap to mine, and I straighten. That's the second time my tongue has run away since entering this room. Maybe it's something in the air. One of the props boxes probably had some weird shit in that's giving off fumes, clouding my judgment.

"Night security?"

I shake my head. "They don't come on shift for another two hours."

This is what I get for playing Mr. Nice Guy and letting the crew knock off early. I knew there was a reason I never usually do anything remotely charitable like that.

"Damn it." She blows out a breath and looks at the ceiling.

My shoulders tighten. She couldn't look any less thrilled about being locked in here with me than if she were tied to a subway track at rush hour.

"Sorry if your inability to read and remember a memo makes you late for your date, or whatever it is you had planned for tonight."

I take in her fitted black dress, which hugs her curves and stops below her knees. She's re-styled her hair into soft waves. It was tied up when I saw her earlier.

Shona's eyes flash with what looks like amusement for the first time since she came in.

"Drinks at Geode."

Geode is a bar in Hollywood that a lot of film industry professionals go to. It's exclusive, concealed, and free from paparazzi.

It's also dark and sultry with walls that glitter like a cave, hence its name.

The perfect place to sit in a low-lit booth, close with a date.

"Well, you look... you..." I run my thumb over my lips. "He's very lucky."

And a bastard. He's a lucky bastard.

She smiles; the flash in her eyes transforming into a radiant glow.

"So..." I tear my eyes away from hers and force myself not to glance at the swell of her cleavage.

Her nipples are hard beneath the thin fabric.

Fuck.

I clear my throat and pretend to find something interesting on an upside-down box label to avoid looking at her.

"Well, we might as well do something to pass the time while we're stuck in here." She stands and pushes the boxes on top of the table to one side so there's room next to her.

"There's room for another." She motions to the tabletop as she slides back onto it.

I hesitate for a moment before walking over and sitting next to her.

The aroma of beautiful flowers fills my nostrils, and I shuffle against the hard surface to get comfortable.

"What would you be doing tonight, then? If we weren't locked in here with Chuckie's evil cousin?" She tilts her chin toward a clown costume hanging on the end of a rail we used in a Halloween episode.

I chuckle, then stop, drawing a curious look from her.

"Going over tomorrow's schedule."

"You ever heard the saying, *All work and no play—*"

"Makes Trent very successful at what he does."

Shona's eyes meet mine and the corners of her lips curl up.

"We need to film the scenes we missed today. Delays cost money." I exhale and roll my head side to side to release the tension in my neck.

"We'll get back on schedule. We always do with you as director." She lets out an unamused laugh.

"What's the tone for?"

"Tone?" She picks at a piece of lint on the front of her dress and brushes her hand down over her breast, dusting it away.

"Come on. You know." Her brows lift as she waits for me to say something.

I don't.

"Fine." She folds her arms and tips her head back to the ceiling, mumbling something about having to look for another job in the morning. "Okay." She looks into my eyes, that intoxicating copper halo in hers holding me captive.

"I meant that as a compliment. I've never worked on a set that runs so efficiently before. You..." She purses her lips. "You're organized, and driven, and brilliant at what you do."

Heat swells in my chest.

"But..."

"But?"

"Well, you're also difficult. You stomp around the set like a child having a tantrum. You shout when you don't get your own way. You expect people to be mind readers. You—"

"I don't."

"You do."

"I don't expect them to be mind readers. I just expect them to do their job properly. I need to be able to *trust* people to do it right."

I press my thumb and forefinger into my eyes and rub until it stings.

I'm saying too much.

Trust.

Way to go, Trent. Pour your fucking heart out so she can tell the rest of the crew tomorrow and you'll be a laughingstock. Again.

When I open my eyes, Shona is looking at me pointedly with an arched brow.

"Sorry," I say for the third time since coming into the room.

What the hell is wrong with me?

She leans against the wall.

"It's not easy when you have your trust and faith in people broken." Her voice is kind, which makes the muscles in my shoulders tighten.

She knows. Of course, she knows. The whole of LA—damn it, the entire world—knows what a colossal betrayal of trust I went through nine months ago when my ex-fiancée, Claudia, left me for my best friend and business partner, Ewan. They'd been fucking behind my back for months.

I was more bothered about losing my friendship with Ewan and the business we'd built together than Claudia. What does that say about me?

Since then, I've worked myself to the bone, building the business back up, clawing back the savings I had to use to buy Ewan out of his share. And I've done it. Alongside some huge projects I've been involved with, acting as guest director on this season of *Steel Force* has been my catapult into being the most sought-after guy for special effects in the industry.

I'm at the top of my game.

And it's fucking lonely up here.

"No, you're right, it isn't," I say in a gentle voice.

We sit in silence for a while, not a single noise from outside to indicate we will get out soon.

"What made you choose makeup?" I ask, wishing to break the quiet, even though it isn't uncomfortable. Shona's strangely calming. Maybe it's her perfume.

But I want to know the answer.

I want to know more about her.

About this woman who has no problem telling me I have a 'tone' and am like a tantruming child. No one has ever spoken so frankly.

My mother would like her.

"Would you believe I wanted to work for NASA?" She laughs as I jerk back in surprise. "Not necessarily going into space, but on the ground. I've always been fascinated by the solar system and planets. I can name all the constellations."

"I'm sure you could have worked there if that's what you'd chosen." I take in her air of calm elegance. The fire in her eyes.

I've no doubt she can achieve whatever she wants. With some people, you can just tell. There's something about them. Something extra driving them. You can see the determination in their eyes, taste it in their presence. Like the actors in this town. Some have what it takes. Others don't.

Shona does.

I'd bet my life on it.

"Maybe." A joyless smile passes over her lips. "But I chose this path instead. I dreamed of space. Yet now, it's all about details and intricacy." She turns to face me. "If I tell you something, will it stay in this room?"

"Of course."

She sighs, pursing her lips as if she's mulling over whether to share.

"I keep my word, Shona." It makes her glance at me, and she nods.

"Okay... My stepdad used to beat my mom. He was younger than her, but bigger. A lot bigger. I learned to do makeup so I could help her hide the bruises. I got good at it from an early age."

"I'm sorry," is all I can think to reply with.

She studies me, her eyes sweeping over my face, and the overwhelming urge to kiss her fires into my thoughts like a cannon.

"Thank you. It was hard seeing that happen to my mom. She would do anything for those she loves. But she loved the wrong person, and he exploited her feelings for him, her spirit."

"Are they still—?"

"Together?" She shakes her head, her eyes leaving my face, and I instantly wish she was still looking at me. "No. My brother, Josh, grew up. He was the same size as Keith by the time he was fifteen. Josh came home one night when Keith had Mom against the wall by her throat, and he beat the shit out of Keith. I think he would have killed him if I hadn't been there to stop him. I didn't want to lose him to prison for protecting us."

"Us?" A cold chill slithers up my spine as images of a young Shona suffering harm at the hands of a man flood my brain.

"He'd sometimes push me around. But Mom always put herself between us. She took the brunt of it."

She rubs her hands up and down her arms, and I grab the nearest coat—an FBI costume jacket—from the wardrobe rail and wrap it around her shoulders.

"He never came back after that night. Made a hell of a fuss leaving. Shouting and cursing. Saying we'd all be dead the next time he saw us. It was all empty threats. He was a bully who finally had someone his own size to contend with. That was years ago. I haven't seen him since. He could be dead, for all I know."

"I hope he is. Cleanse the planet, one asshole at a time," I hiss.

Shona laughs, the sound like fucking music to my ears. My breath hitches in my throat as our eyes meet and the halo in hers shimmers.

I smile.

"You should smile more." Her laugh leaves her in a peaceful sigh as she studies my face again.

It should feel intrusive. The way she's looking at me so deeply, like she can draw out my inner thoughts if only she looks hard enough.

Yet, it feels... nice.

Who am I kidding? It feels fucking incredible to have someone looking at me like I'm not the biggest jerk to work with in the history of Hollywood. I know my reputation. Like I said, it doesn't bother me.

But Shona looking at me with a smile spreading over her pretty lips is a feeling I haven't felt in a long time. Not since Claudia. Actually, not even then.

I reach forward and adjust the jacket around her. My hand skims her neck as I straighten the collar.

Rough meets silk.

Temptation meets the thin line between professional decency and downright inappropriateness.

She's one of my team members. And she's locked inside a small room without windows with me.

What kind of a creeper am I?

"Trent…"

A rattling at the door, and the sound of a key in the lock outside, breaks our eye contact. The door opens and one of the night security team peers inside.

"Wasn't expecting anyone to be in here, but I saw the light underneath the door."

"About fucking time." I jump off the desk, incensed at my complete lack of control around Shona, and stride over to the open doorway.

"Thank you," Shona says behind me as she follows me out.

There's a pause, and I'm sure if I turned around, I would see a look pass between the two, conveying what an asshole they think I am.

I clear my throat and turn to face the guard. "Thank you."

His eyes bulge at my sudden infusion of manners. It's no secret that the crew call me 'Sparky' because of my sharp, abrasive nature.

"Thank you," I repeat once more. "We could have been in there a long time. And Shona was getting cold."

She's taken off the FBI jacket and her goosebumps have disappeared.

She smiles at the guard and something bitter coils in my stomach. His eyes are fixated leisurely on the swell of her breasts.

"It's no problem. Hey, why don't I give you my number, then if it happens again, you can call me." He grins at her.

"How about you tell the maintenance team to fix the damn door." I glare at him, my hand seeking the base of Shona's back and guiding her down the hallway toward the exit before he reacts.

Once we get out into the evening air, I remove my hand and we walk to the parking lot in silence.

"Can I give you a ride to your date?"

I point my keys at my shiny black Maclaren Spider and hit the button. The doors lift at the sides, opening toward the sky.

"It's the bat mobile." Shona stares at it. In awe or distaste; I can't tell from her straight face.

"Well, you called me a child earlier. Makes sense I should have some big toys."

"Big toys, huh?"

Is she flirting?

She climbs into her car, her long, high-heeled legs folding inside behind her.

"Have a good evening," she calls, giving me a wave.

"Enjoy your date," I counter. My back tenses, unease bristling throughout my body as she clicks her seatbelt in.

"Oh, I will." Her eyes glitter as she closes the door.

I'm left standing in the parking lot as her taillights fade into the distance.

What the fuck has gotten into me?

Chapter 4
Shona

When I arrive at work the following morning, Gloria is grinning at me like the bird who caught the canary.

"What?" I walk into the makeup trailer and place my bag on the table, then fish out a hair tie and gather my hair into a ponytail.

It's going to be a full day of filming. We have yesterday's scenes to do, as well as what was originally on today's schedule. I'm glad it wasn't a late one last night. But I'm equally glad I didn't miss drinks with a couple of girls I worked with on a small indie production with last year. They're both on permanent contracts over at *The After Hours Show*, Hollywood's top chat show. Apparently, the show's been trying to book Jay Anderson for months, but the shooting schedule here at *Steel Force* is just too intense for him to commit.

"Nothing." Gloria is still grinning. "Just, thank you, that's all. I can see properly this morning."

My brow creases in confusion as she points at a lamp that's appeared overnight. She flicks it on, illuminating the space with bright light.

"Don't thank me. Maintenance must have brought it." I inspect the lamp. The large head swivels three hundred and sixty degrees. It's what we need until the new mirrors come.

"If by maintenance, you mean a certain Mr. Forde, then you would be correct."

"What?" I gape at her, as she nods her head, looking smug.

"Brought it by himself before you arrived. Said it was in the props room taking up space and he needed it out."

My mind whizzes as I flip my gaze from Gloria to the lamp and then back to Gloria again.

"I'm surprised too. Sparky has earned himself a point." She pops a brow at me as I open up my kit and start setting up.

"Yes. Well, it's our gain, I guess."

Gloria smirks, her eyes glued to my face. "Sure is."

She hums as we prepare for the day.

Trent brought that lamp this morning? It must be what he was looking for in the props room last night. Before we got locked in. Before he gave me the jacket and his fingers brushed over my jaw.

Those fingers.

Is it possible to feel an electric current when someone touches you? Feel one so deeply, coursing through your body from one small connection of skin, as though you've been turned off your entire life, and someone plugged you in and flicked the switch?

Because that's exactly how it felt when Trent's skin dusted across mine.

A sensation, unexpected, yet the most exhilarating shock to my system.

I shake my head, scattering my thoughts and pushing Trent firmly to the back. So he brought us a lamp.

Big deal.

He's still abrasive and rude and... *misunderstood?*

I didn't imagine the hurt in his eyes when he mentioned his ex-fiancée betraying him with his best friend. How low can you get? Still, it isn't a reason for stomping around like an overgrown sullen child when you don't get your way. A fact I distinctly recall sharing my views about with him last night.

Shit. My shoulders stiffen as I lay out my brushes. I could easily be looking for another job this morning as a result of being so frank. I never used to be this way. But the second that my brother's fist connected with Keith's face that notorious night, it's like a lock was broken open.

I always promised myself I will speak up. I'll never let anyone silence my voice again. Because seeing Mom, and what he did to her... I knew I never wanted to feel afraid again. We spent years hiding her bruises and tiptoeing around Keith to survive. It's what we had to do. And I understand. Mom was scared for herself and her two children. Scared of a monster who was bigger and stronger than her.

But it made me vow to never stay quiet again when I don't agree with something. I'm honest to a fault now. A trait that sometimes backfires. Thankfully, it hasn't right now.

"I wonder what his house is like?"

"Huh?"

"Trent's." Gloria's eyes gleam. "We'll find out next Friday…. at the party," she adds as I stare at her, blank-faced.

"Party?"

"End of season blow-out!" Gloria dances on her toes.

"At Trent's house?"

"Well, duh. It's all everyone was talking about on the way home last night. You'd have heard it all if you left when we did."

I avoid her gaze. She's known me long enough to know when I'm hiding something. As far as Gloria is concerned, I stayed late to go to the props room for extra fake blood for today's special effect gunshot wound we need to create. She has no idea I spent half the evening locked inside it with Trent.

That would give her enough ammo to blast me for weeks. She's already gotten it into her head that he's some dynamo in the sack I should experience.

It's better if she doesn't know.

It's better that no-one does.

"I wonder if he has a red room like that character—"

"Why don't you ask him for a tour," I cut in, my lips quirking. "Perhaps, he will oblige at the party."

"Better yet"—she narrows her eyes at me—"why don't you ask him for one? End the season on a real bang." Her brows shoot up her forehead.

Here we go. I try to fight my smile. I know exactly what's coming.

"Get yourself some action, tell me if I'm right about him. I bet he has a huge—"

Ralph walks in, two steaming cups in his hands, saving me from whichever word of choice Gloria was about to scar my ears with.

Wrapping up filming for the season shoots by, and there's a buzz of excitement and achievement bouncing around as everyone leaves the set on Friday. We still need to film the season trailer next week and some promotional footage. But all the episodes are done.

It feels amazing.

I grin and wave at one of the girls from wardrobe as she heads to her car. Trent's shiny, black Maclaren is still parked in the lot. I wouldn't expect him to have left yet, even if he is hosting a party at his house tonight. He's always one of the final ones on set; it's part of being Director.

He's been intense these past ten days. Wrapping up filming must be both stressful and exhilarating for a director. Finally seeing all your ideas come to fruition. Wondering if you've nailed it, if your vision has been executed to the best of everyone's abilities.

He's been so busy, barking out orders in his usual manner that I haven't had a chance to thank him for the lamp. He's been constantly surrounded by members of the team needing him or asking for his guidance.

Despite all his brashness, he is respected. He knows what he's doing. No-one does it like him. This has easily been the most well-run, efficient set I've ever worked on, and I know I'm not alone in thinking that. And he's seemed a touch less snappy recently. Intense still, but warmer. He was standing with one of the lighting guys earlier, head tilted back, a deep, sexy laugh emanating from his broad chest. The curl of his dark hair peeked out from below his ball cap and his eyes crinkled in the sunlight. He had a gray top on that stretched over his corded forearms where he'd pushed the sleeves up, and a rolled-up script shoved into the back pocket of his dark denim jeans.

Jeans that hugged a muscular ass and thick, strong thighs.

I noticed.

Trent Forde might be one grumpy asshole. But he's also brilliant, the best at what he does, and... *hotter than the devil.*

───── *ele* ─────

"Is it like you expected?" Gloria asks as we walk across the marble floor of the giant, double-height entryway, complete with dual sweeping staircases running up either side.

"It's..." I search for the right word to describe Trent's house, I mean, mansion. Hell, I mean palace.

This is the second walk we've done around the ground floor. Gloria's hand has tightened around my arm, her nails pressing into my skin every time she spots something new and incredible. Which has been every few minutes.

"I knew it would be an outdoor pool," she gushes as we head past a long hallway table covered in framed pictures of Trent with various recognizable Hollywood faces. He's smiling in them with perfect teeth, and radiant, glowing eyes.

He loves his job. This world.

There's a picture of him and Jay Anderson fooling around. It looks like Jay has thrown a load of ice cubes down Trent's back, and he's yanked his t-shirt up to get them out, flashing his washboard abs and golden skin.

I could be wrong, but looking at all the pictures, I would bet my most expensive brush set these were all taken before his fiancée left him. It's the lightness in his stance, the lack of tension usually present in his shoulders, the slight set of his jaw that's there every day now.

He carries the deceit around with him like a dark force, woven into his skin.

One picture, almost hidden at the back, catches my eye. I recognize the two people with him immediately. The woman, long blonde hair, baby blue eyes, curves and sex appeal like a pin-up, has her arms around Trent, her head resting against his shoulder.

Claudia.

And the man on his other side with a broad, dazzling smile on his lips, shaved head, and a neck just as thick.

Ewan. His ex-best friend, who Claudia cheated on him with.

Fury licks at my core. How could they? How could anyone do that to anyone? I know how it feels to experience the ugly the side of the human spirit. But to be betrayed by your fiancée and best friend?

For god's sake.

I stare at the photographs for a second longer before Gloria tugs me through to the kitchen.

"See!" She points to where an entire glass wall has been opened up, revealing a lit deck area and large garden with a shimmering pool surrounded by palms. "Fifty bucks says people will be swimming before the night is out."

"I didn't bring my bathing suit."

"No one did." Gloria beams as Jay Anderson walks into the room from the garden with two other actors from the show. The three look like a men's fitness advert, all bronzed skin, and clothing showcasing the outline of their muscles. "Let's hope those guys kick it off." She giggles and pulls us over to a counter, backed with tall glass shelves, lit up with neon blue lights.

"He has a bar in his kitchen?" I stare at the modern installation as Gloria fixes us two drinks and hands me a margarita.

"Shona, he has everything." She waves at Jay and the other two guys and grins as they head over to join us.

I sip my drink, thinking about the cozy trio in the photograph.

Everything?

Somehow, I doubt Trent would agree.

Half an hour and two more margaritas later, I signal to Gloria and the guys that I'm going to find the bathroom.

I walk out of the kitchen, back past the table with all the photographs on and into the impressive entryway. The house is buzzing with energy, and what seems like half of Hollywood are here, flouncing about, drinks in hand, chatting and laughing, air-kissing and admiring one another's outfits. Loud music pumps out from a built-in speaker system. I peek into the large living space off the foyer. The furniture has been pushed against the walls, making way for a throng of bodies grinding against one another.

It's odd. I've seen the entire *Steel Force* cast and crew since I arrived, plus a load of other people. But one person is missing.

Trent.

Why have a giant party in your own house and not even come out to see your guests? It's possible I've missed him. But at his height, and with the air of quiet dominance he has about him, I doubt that's the case.

I'd sense it in the air before I even saw him if he walked into the room I was in.

A line of three girls against one wall draws my attention. They're waiting for the bathroom. There's probably another one out near the kitchen, or in the pool house. But that would mean going back through the kitchen and getting drawn back into the conversation with Gloria and the guys. When I left, she was asking them for fitness tips, grabbing a good feel of their hard stomachs and giant arms for 'research'.

Nobody can refuse her. She can get away with anything.

I run my hand over the smooth, inky black handrail at the base of one of the twin staircases. The line of girls still hasn't moved, and another girl has joined at the back.

I'm sure Trent won't mind if I go upstairs to the bathroom.

I walk up, my red stilettos clacking against the ebony wood.

The upstairs must have an unspoken out-of-bounds agreement to it, because it's deserted. I walk into the main hallway, door after closed door lining either side of the wide space.

On the walls are framed prints of iconic TV and movie scenes, all famous for their special effects.

Trent must have worked on these.

I try the first door I pass. I don't want to be up here longer than necessary because it will look like I'm snooping if anyone sees me.

A large, luxurious marble bathroom with a walk-in rainfall shower and a giant freestanding bathtub greets me, and I can't stop my smile as I step inside. I freshen up, shaking out my hair and re-applying my red lipstick before smoothing down my white mini dress. It's nice to wear something bright and not have it covered in a day's worth of makeup and fake blood. Mine and Gloria's go-to work wardrobe consists of black t-shirts and black pants, sometimes a skirt.

I open the door and walk out, and curiosity gets the better of me as a sound comes from behind another closed door. The voice is deep, muffled, and alone. Either they're talking to themselves, or they're on the phone.

I hover in the hallway as a deep rumble of a laugh rings out. Heat spreads up my spine, pinning me to the spot.

Trent.

I'd know that sinful laugh anywhere. I may have only heard it twice, but that's all that was needed.

Once you hear a sound like that, so raw, so confident, so... *sexy*, you never forget it.

The laugh stops and the door flies open. A hot, solid body stalks out, crashing straight into me.

"Ouch!"

Large hands wrap around the bare skin of my upper arms, steadying me. Deep brown eyes hold mine, that dark hair with a slight curl to it filling the edges of my vision like a darkened halo around his face.

"Shona, I'm sorry. Are you okay?"

I breathe in slowly, the electric current surging in my body from the prolonged skin-to-skin contact.

"Did I hurt you, are you...?" Trent moves both of his hands from my arms and cups my face, staring into my eyes.

I swallow as I struggle to rein in whatever this weird sensation is.

"I'm fine," I finally whisper, searching his eyes as they soften, and his shoulders relax.

He exhales and drops his gaze to my lips.

"Trent...?"

My heart jumps into my throat as he swipes the pad of his thumb over my bottom lip and his jaw clenches.

"Trent?" I repeat.

Chapter 5
Trent

"Trent...?"

Her soft voice snaps me back to reality, and I pull my hands away from her face with lightning speed.

I shove them deep into my pockets so I don't fuck up and touch her again.

I'm an idiot. What the hell am I doing? She's up here alone, and I'm grabbing her like that?

"I'm sorry, I just... you looked a little shaken. I slammed right into you."

I try not to let my eyes drop over the tight white dress she has on as images of slamming into her in a different manner flood my brain.

I need air. Or a hormone blocker... or something.

She studies me; that copper ring in her eyes blazing with an intensity I wish I could read.

Is she thinking I'm a jerk who can't keep his hands to himself?

Fuck, she's beautiful. Captivating—the hair, the lips, the breasts—Jesus, the breasts. It's the say-it-like-it-is attitude I was introduced to that night in the props room. And the strength that radiates from her. Like a forcefield.

"Why are you up here? You're missing your own party." She crosses her arms over her chest, pushing her breasts higher.

I groan involuntarily, but she doesn't notice.

I hold her gaze, the copper ring glittering back at me in amusement.

"You're upstairs in *my* house, and you're asking me what *I'm* doing here?" I tap a finger against my chest, and her eyes follow it, before sweeping over my shoulders and back to my face.

She purses those enticing red lips. "I came to use the bathroom. The line downstairs was four deep."

I try my hardest to think pure thoughts that won't convey what I'm thinking to my facial expression, as she adds, "It's really beautiful by the way... the whole house is."

"Thank you." A smile spreads over my lips and Shona's eyes dart to them and back up.

This house is one of my biggest achievements, bought after I made my first fifty million. The fact I barely use half of it most of the time hasn't put my mother off telling every soul she meets that her son lives next door to one of the country's retired presidents.

Even if that isn't true.

"Oh! I wanted to thank you for the lamp you brought to the trailer. I haven't seen you properly to tell you."

"You're welcome, Shona. Is it okay for you?"

She doesn't answer.

"How was your date at Geode the other week?" I ask, trying a new tactic to illicit a reaction from her.

She blinks at me. "There was no date. I'm single."

There, just like that.

Straight to the point, no messing about.

Is she merely stating facts? Or is this an invitation?

She fidgets under my gaze, tucking her hair behind her ear.

From the few interactions with her, I can tell she isn't easily embarrassed or shy, yet the way her pulse is fluttering beneath the skin of her neck at double speed makes me wonder if she is okay.

Maybe I bumped her harder than I thought—

"Fuck it," she mutters, then steps forward and presses herself against my chest.

She presses her lips to mine.

And kisses me.

If I were a true gentleman, the sweet taste of alcohol on her breath would have me pulling back to check she's sure about what's happening. And I do... or at least, I try. But she wraps her arms around my neck, a breathy sigh caught in her throat as she clutches me tight.

And all bets are off.

My hands whip out of my pants faster than a clapperboard, and I sink them into the hair, pulling her closer.

Our lips move together like they've been performing this dance for years. The perfect pressure, the perfect urgency... *just perfect.*

"You're a great kisser," Shona murmurs, parting her lips and inviting me to taste her even deeper.

"You make me want to kiss you everywhere," I reply, sliding my tongue inside her mouth.

She grips on to me. I back us against the wall, blood racing around my body and settling in my hardening dick. I tilt her head back and devour every millimeter of her soft red lips.

She tastes sweet, addictive, and dangerous.

Everything I haven't allowed into my life in months.

Yet, I can't stop myself. There could be a neon sign saying, *Impending doom this way*, and I would be first in line to get the early-bird ticket and dive into oblivion.

As long as I can keep kissing her.

Our kiss grows urgent, and I groan into her mouth, my raging hard-on sticking into her stomach with all the subtlety of a nuclear missile.

"Trent." She pulls back, panting, her lipstick smeared around her lips.

My pulse picks up at the sight of her flushed face.

"That was... I was..." She stares at me, her fingertips hovering over her lips.

The thought she might be about to apologize or try to take back what happened has my gut tensing.

Don't say it was mistake. Nothing that feels that good can be a mistake.

"Have dinner with me tomorrow night?" I breathe out in a rush, still catching my breath, my body alight with desire and anticipation, every small hair on the back of my neck ramrod straight.

"Tomorrow...?" She frowns.

"Tomorrow," I confirm, swallowing hard, as I wait for her to think up an excuse. I'm her boss. That would be the obvious one, even though there are no rules in either of our contracts that say we can't—

"Okay."

"Okay?"

"I mean, yes, please." She smiles, her eyes glittering.

And just like that, my new favorite color is copper.

No fucking doubt about it.

Chapter 6
Shona

SEVEN P.M. THE FOLLOWING evening, a driver in a black suit, who looks out of place in my neighborhood, comes and rings the bell.

"Miss West?" He smiles as I answer the door.

I nod, taking in the sleek black town car parked at the curb over his shoulder.

"I'm Sam. Mr. Forde asked that I accompany you to his house. You have dinner plans with him?"

"Yes, thank you." I grab my purse and follow him down the path to the car.

I slide into the cool leather interior and tuck my dress around my legs. Sam closes the door and then climbs into the driver's seat.

Maybe we're going back to Trent's house to pick him up. The set was closed today since we all had a day off. But he works on different projects, so perhaps, his day ran late and he's at home getting changed.

I make small talk to fill the silence. Sam tells me he's worked for Trent as his driver for several years, even before the Claudia and Ewan scandal, not that he mentions it, but I work out the timeline in my head and know he must have been with Trent when that shit went down.

I ask if 'Sparky' is as much of a perfectionist at home as he is on set, and his nickname draws a throaty laugh from Sam. By the time we pull up at Trent's house—which looks bigger in broad daylight—I know all about Sam, his two sisters, one brother, and the fact his mom has a cat called Kanga, because it likes to bounce like a kangaroo around the house.

"Have a lovely evening." Sam gives me a friendly wink as he lets me in the front door and then retreats, leaving me standing in the giant, double height, marble entryway.

"Shona?"

Goosebumps scatter up my spine in reaction to Trent's voice as he appears from the kitchen. He gently kisses me on one cheek, his hand cupping my elbow.

"You look beautiful." He draws back before I can lose myself in the aroma of his aftershave—clean, heady, masculine.

"Thank you." I tilt my chin to meet his eyes. I'm tall, but even in heels, his six-foot-five frame towers above me.

"Come." His hand rests over my lower back, and I enjoy the vibration his strong fingers create through my body.

He steers me across the foyer toward the kitchen.

I pause as we pass the table with all the framed photographs on.

The one of him, Claudia, and Ewan has gone.

Trent follows my gaze, and as if reading my mind, says, "It's when she's cleaning. She keeps putting it out, my—"

"Housekeeper?" I say as he slides open the drawer in the table and taps his finger against the glass of the absent frame placed inside.

His lips curl into a sad smile.

"It's not intentional. She has problems with her memory. I know she'll have to stop doing things around the house for me soon and need a full-time caregiver. But I enjoy our talks and holding on to what time we have before that becomes inevitable. That's selfish, isn't it? Holding on to the past because what lies in the future is too damn terrifying to think about."

I stare into his eyes, the faint lines around them deepening as if caught in a moment. A memory of a time now gone.

I can't believe I ever thought Trent Forde was an abrasive workaholic who cared for little else than his career when it's obvious he is so much more.

He's a man with a giant heart. A man who's had his trust abused by people who weren't worthy of having him in their lives.

He slides the drawer shut, and Ewan and Claudia's deceitful faces disappear from sight.

"I don't think that's selfish. That's human. Caring about someone else is the least selfish thing in the world."

A warm ball grows in my chest as Trent runs a hand around the back of his neck, embarrassed.

I don't think I've ever seen him look less than one hundred percent in control and focused on work before.

Except last night in the upstairs hallway. But even then, he wasn't like this. It's like I'm glimpsing the soft layers beneath his tough, outer shell.

And I want more.

I want to peel them away, one by one, and uncover the man underneath.

"Will Sam be taking us to dinner?" I ask as Trent guides me into the kitchen.

"No. I thought we'd eat here, if that's okay with you? Although, I must confess, I didn't make it myself. The best restaurant this side of Hollywood delivers." He chuckles as he leads me outside. The terrace surrounding the pool is lit up with fairy lights. It's a warm evening. I can only imagine how incredible the set-up for two will look once the sun goes down.

"Wow, this is..." My eyes rake over the expanse of manicured gardens, which I never saw properly last night. An intoxicating scent of honeysuckle from the nearby billowing bushes drifts over, and my body relaxes as the evening sun washes over me in soft waves. "... Really quite unique," I finish as I continue my exploration of the beautiful space.

"I think real beauty lies in the unique," Trent says, his deep voice sending a ripple of energy dancing through me, flooding my cheeks with warmth.

I'm not sure he's talking about the garden anymore. "Come. Sit."

He pulls out a chair for me, and I sink into the seat. He pours me a glass of champagne, then does the same for himself before sitting opposite me. I take in his light blue shirt, the sleeves rolled up, exposing his tanned forearms.

He looks relaxed.

He's never relaxed.

It suits him.

We spend the next hour and a half talking and laughing over the most delicious pad thai and coconut dessert I've ever tasted. Trent has loosened up more as the sun has slowly dipped in the sky, taking the last of the day's light with it. Our table is now lit by fairy lights and some candles.

"So, let me get this straight." I point my spoon at him. "She was naked *and* covered in confetti?"

"I swear!" Trent's eyes sparkle, and he throws his hands up either side of his head.

I finish my last mouthful of dessert and place my fork down with a soft moan.

Best dessert ever.

"Why did Jay never tell me this?" My eyes widen at the mental image forming in my head of an enthusiastic fan that got herself into Jay Anderson's trailer and spread herself naked on the floor.

"I think he's still processing it. The confetti had his face printed on it."

"No."

"Yes." He chuckles. "The cleaning team kept finding it in his trailer a week later."

"Oh my god." I laugh. "Has anything like that ever happened to you?"

"Me? No." He shakes his head. "No inventive super-fans in my past."

"No naked woman waiting for you in your trailer?" I raise a brow as I smile at him.

"Not unless you count an ex who was riding my best friend."

The air leaves my lungs, and I stare at his brows, knitting over his darkening eyes.

"That's how you found out? They were in *your* trailer."

He clears his throat, his eyes dropping to the stem of his champagne flute as he runs his fingers up and down the glass.

"Mine got more sun than Ewan's. It was warmer. Apparently, that's a necessity if you're going to be screwing when the rest of the cast are shooting an early morning scene."

"I'm so sorry, Trent. That was a shitty thing they did." I take in the twisted grimace on his lips. He still thinks about it, it's obvious. And why wouldn't he? His best friend and his fiancée?

I can't think of much worse.

"Yeah." He exhales heavily. "It sure was. I just regret not acting sooner. I knew, suspected something, but never did a thing. I promised myself afterward that

I would never not act in future. Not when I think something's wrong."

My heart sinks.

He blames himself.

"Do you miss them?"

He takes a few moments to answer, and regret swirls in my stomach at being so thoughtless and prying into something that has nothing to do with me.

"One more than the other," he answers finally.

We fall silent for a few minutes, and I imagine how much it must hurt to have planned a future with someone. A life. Building a family together. For them to then crush it by sleeping with your best friend.

No wonder he misses it, the lost dream.

Trent pulls his chair around so he's sitting next to me and then takes his phone from his pocket and taps the screen.

"Let me show you something I've been working on."

"Okay." His joy is clear by the light returning to his eyes, the way it does whenever we use a new special effect on set.

He's back in full Trent Forde mode.

And it's captivating.

"Watch." He tips his chin toward the sky as it lights up with the *Steel Force* logo. A second later, it's sucked away as though swallowed by a black hole, and an explosion of stars replaces it, showering down to earth through the night sky. They look so real I want to reach out and touch one.

"That's amazing! How do you do that?" I gasp and turn to him.

"A mix of holographics and drones."

"And you programed all of them to work from your phone?"

"Yeah." He shrugs like it's the simplest thing in the world.

"Now I can see why you have a mansion with half of Hollywood knocking at your door for you to direct for them."

He laughs softly. "It's what I love doing, Shona. That's all."

I take my gaze away from his deep brown eyes and rest my head back in my chair, staring into the sky.

"You can see Orion tonight." I point up at the star formation, smiling.

Trent follows my gaze as truths spill out of me. Champagne does that. I should have stopped after the first glass.

"Mom, Josh, and I used to lie in our back yard when my stepdad was out drinking, and we'd stargaze. We'd imagine we had a rocket and could fly off into space, leave the world behind and go on an adventure." My chest deflates as I remember how much I loved those nights. Until Keith staggered back through the door and ruined it. He ruined everything.

"That's why you dreamed of working at NASA?"

Trent's eyes are fixed on my face. I don't know what it is, but the way he's looking at me, filled with a burning intensity, has me staring back with equal raw emotion as I fight to keep my voice steady.

"Yes," I whisper.

"I think what you did for your mom means more than all the stars in the universe. We only get that time with them once."

I swallow, my eyes stinging.

He remembers me telling him about covering up my mom's bruises for her.

"That sounds sort of romantic coming from the most abrasive man in Hollywood," I tease, enjoying the way his eyes crease at the corners as he considers my words.

"You're right. I have an asshole reputation to maintain. Better quit while I'm ahead."

I study him, the dark curl of his hair against his collar, the strong planes of his cheekbones, the stubble on his jaw.

I rest a hand on his forearm and twist to face him.

"Your secret's safe with me, Sparky." I bite my bottom lip, waiting for his reaction. I'm pushing him out of his grump-ass controlled comfort zone. And I know he's able to step outside of it.

He turns his dark eyes, diving into mine with no mercy, reaching deep into my soul and showing it he sees me. It steals the breath straight from my body in one rush. A trace of a smile dusts his lips, and he whispers, "*You're* safe with me.

Trent Forde.

Intense. Passionate... Devastating.

Everything that would usually make me feel anything but safe.

But in this moment, I couldn't care less.

All I want is to see what lies beyond. Beyond the gruff exterior. Beyond the outer shell of the most sought-after guy in Hollywood.

Just beyond.

His eyes drop to my lips, and he leans close enough that the coconut scent of his breath ghosts over my cheek.

"Stay."

"What?"

"Stay the night with me, Shona. Stay and let me appreciate every part of you."

My breath stalls at his forwardness. He lifts his hand, tucking a strand of loose hair away from my eyes, then curls his palm around the back of my flushed neck. He licks his lips, his fingertips stroking the delicate skin down the edge of my windpipe, making me shudder.

"Say you will."

I open my mouth to respond. I knew from the kiss last night that there's an attraction here. You don't have a kiss like that if you aren't both attracted to one another.

But to hear him state it so confidently. So blatantly.

I don't think I've ever heard anything hotter.

He moves his thumb to my lips, swiping over them as he leans closer, his lips grazing my own.

"Shona..." he rumbles, sending an influx of butterflies to rage a war inside my stomach. "Agree to be mine tonight."

My body screams out my answer, pumping it in my ears with the sound of my pulse, drumming it against my chest with the pounding of my heart.

I slide a hand up onto his chest and turn my cheek, tracing over his thumb with my lips.

The curl of his smile as I hold his gaze tells me he understands perfectly.

There's only one thing I want to be tonight.

His.

Chapter 7
Trent

THE SILK OF HER dress pools like a scarlet puddle over the carpet as she steps out of it.

I pull her back into my arms.

"Trent," she murmurs, sending shockwaves coursing through my body as I dust my lips over the soft, silky skin on her neck and bite gently.

I reach around and flick her bra, unfastening it so it falls away.

"My god..." I hook my thumbs down either side of her panties and slide them over her hips, before letting them drop to the floor. "You're beautiful."

I can't hide the raging erection fighting its way over my boxers waistband as I take in her full breasts with rich, dusky pink nipples. I stride forward, closing the distance and pulling her back into my arms. I tilt her chin up so I can kiss her again. A kiss as deep and as full of desire as each one we've shared since I led her to my bedroom, her hand wrapped tightly in mine.

"Yes," she murmurs against my lips as I take one breast inside my palm and tug at her pebbled nipple.

"You like that?" I lean down and draw the tight peak in through my lips.

She arches toward me with a cry, her hands dropping to squeeze my shoulders.

"Mm."

"Tell me with words, Shona."

Her lips part as she draws in a breath. "I should have known you'd be bossy."

I chuckle, then suck harder.

"Fuck," she hisses.

"Something tells me you wouldn't take kindly to being bossed around by anyone." I smile and move to her other breast, lavishing it with the same attention.

"Maybe," she muses, her fingernails digging into my skin, the subtle sting speaking directly to my dick and sending more blood racing to it.

"Maybe?" I continue sucking her nipple, swirling my tongue around it again to see if she shudders like last time.

She does.

"Maybe I could enjoy…" I swirl my tongue, then flick it over her. "Maybe I could enjoy being bossed around… if it was by you."

Fuck yes. My dick strains to the point of pain.

"Maybe," she continues, "you'd enjoy me bossing you around too."

I groan, then stand so I can hold the back of her neck and claim her mouth with my tongue again.

"What would you have me do?" I grind out between kisses. Our lips never break contact as I press my body against hers until my rock-hard dick is pressed into her stomach.

"I don't know," she whispers. "Maybe have you show me what special effects your tongue can do."

I tighten my grasp on her neck, pulling back to stare into her eyes, as hot desire pools low in my groin. The copper circle blazes around her pupils, brighter than the stars we saw outside.

"You want to take turns at giving orders? I'll go first." I arch a brow at her as I walk her backward to the bed, tearing off my boxers on the way. I lie on it so I can gaze at her. "Now come and put your legs on either side of my face and sit. I'll show you what special effects means."

She smiles as I grab her hand.

"Hurry up." I smirk. "I'm hungry."

A moan escapes from her in a rush as I pull her onto my waiting mouth. My groan echoes around the room as I get my first taste of her.

Sweet as fucking candy. Just how I dreamed.

"I could eat you out all night. You taste incredible."

She whimpers as I spread her thighs wider, encouraging her to grind on my face. I move my head side to side, my eyes damn near rolling back in my head as I suck and lick on her hot skin and swollen clit.

"Trent," she moans above me. She must be close because her inhibitions and reluctance slip away, and she rides my face.

Hard.

Jesus. My cock is weeping all over my stomach, my balls throbbing with the mere idea of blowing my load anywhere near her.

"That's it, Darling. Ride my face." I kiss, lick, and suck her release closer to the surface.

Her thighs tremble.

"Give it to me," I murmur, grasping her hips with both hands and pulling her harder onto my mouth.

"Trent…"

She fists my hair with a hand and rotates her hips, fucking my face with the kind of pure pleasure-loving freedom I've only ever dreamed about a partner showing.

She's strong. I knew that from what she's shared about her past.

But she's also not afraid to go after what she wants.

She jerks her hand, positioning my mouth where she wants it. "Suck my clit again."

And to ask for it.

I circle faster until she bucks, coming hard. I'm rewarded with a squirt of arousal, which coats the lower half of my face, running down my chin.

"Oh wow," she chokes out.

I lap up her orgasm, my cock throbbing. She writhes and tries to put distance between my mouth and her pulsating pussy, but I clamp down on her hips, holding her in place.

"No more… I can't…"

I smile against her. "Oh, Darling… you can, and you will."

Her moans build back up as I continue to tongue her clit, until she's grinding onto my face again. The second time she comes, she curses me, but her tone is laced with desire.

My balls are at a real risk of exploding soon with how fucking turned on I am.

Her face is flushed when I finally loosen my grip on her.

I move her down my body so she's straddling my hips.

"I think I like bossy Shona."

She raises her brows, her dark hair cascading down around her shoulders and spilling over her breasts.

"And I think I like fun, but still super-bossy Sparky," she says, her eyes glittering.

"You do?"

"Trent..."

"Shona." I stroke her hipbones, my cock ramrod straight and leaking pre-cum where it's nestled between her ass cheeks.

She leans down, her breasts pressing against my chest, their weight against me making me moan out loud as she whispers in my ear, "Please tell me fucking me with your cock will make me come that hard as well."

My dick may as well have leaped into my throat from the sudden jerk it gives at her words.

Hell yes! Challenge accepted.

"Why don't you get on your back and spread that pretty pussy for me, and you can find out," I say, pressing a kiss to the column of her throat.

Her eyelids grow hooded as she slides her leg over my body and does as I ask.

I grin.

She likes to be in control as much as she likes to surrender it.

I thought she was special before, but now I know...

She is fucking *unique*.

"Open wider, Darling. Let me see what you've got for me."

Her eyes flash, dropping to where I'm rolling a condom onto my angry cock. Even the brush of the latex sliding down my shaft has my balls pulsating out with the goddamn strength of a rapper's extra bass album.

Shona lies back, her incredible breasts rising and falling as she pants in anticipation. She spreads her legs wide and parts her glistening pussy lips with bloodred fingernails.

Fucking hell.

My heart thrums in my chest. I'm sure this is what the early stages of a heart attack must feel like.

I can't die now.

Please, heart, wait until after. Give me this.

I run one hand over my jaw, breathing deeply, my eyes glued to the plump pink skin, still swollen from where I ate her out so enthusiastically.

"Are you wondering if it'll fit?" Shona drags her eyes away from my sheathed cock that I'm slowly fisting and up to my face. "Because I am."

I tower over her, sliding my hands up each of her arms, positioning them above her head on the mattress. Then I pin her wrists in place beneath one hand.

"Don't worry, Darling." I use my other hand to hook under her knee and spread her further. "We'll make it fit."

A small smile plays on her lips, and I relish the split second it changes to a pleasured O as I push forward into her tight, wet heat.

We stare at each other, lips parted, sharing breath. Gazing. Fitting. Feeling.

I pull back and push forward again, catching her lips in a kiss as she cries out and I fill her to the hilt.

"See? Perfect fit," I murmur into her mouth as she moans around my tongue.

I circle my hips, easing her wider, then pull out and sink back inside. I'm even deeper this time, and as my balls push against her skin, she peels her spine off the bed to get closer.

"You feel fucking incredible," I rasp, building up rhythm with my hips as I fuck her the way I've dreamed about since she first spoke back to me.

I've dreamed about filling her pussy, and then her throat for having the audacity to talk to me like that on my own fucking set.

No one has ever had the nerve.

And nothing has ever gotten me so hard.

Shona moans with each thrust, her delicious tits bouncing with the force that I'm driving into her with.

I can't decide whether to look at them, or the beautiful flush that's overtaken her cheeks as she stares at me with desire.

I pause inside her, dipping my head to suck each nipple. I swirl my tongue around each one and am rewarded with her pussy clenching around me.

"I love your tits," I groan, tearing myself away from them and planting my lips straight back on top of hers. "I swear I could come from just sucking your nipples."

"I swear I could come from you doing that too," she whispers against my mouth as I hitch her leg higher and grind my hips so the flesh above my dick rubs her clit.

"We can try it later. But right now, I want to feel you let go. I want to see how wet you get when you come on my cock," I hiss as I let her wrists go and rise to my knees.

I grab both of her legs and hold them open so I can pump into her.

I stretch her obscenely and drag her back onto me repeatedly, not slowing down for a moment.

Maybe I'm a bastard, but it's been a while. Besides, judging by the blush creeping over her neck and the way her thighs are trembling in my hands, my guess would be she's getting off on it as much as I am.

"You okay?" I check, stroking the skin on her legs with my thumbs as I drive inside her, making her breasts bounce.

Jesus, those tits. I will fuck them later.

"Don't you dare stop. I'm going to come!" she fires back, as she drops her head against the mattress. She grabs the back of my hands on her hips and holds on tight.

Definitely okay then.

The first spasm of her pussy is like a slap to my cock. The second like two hands wrapping around its throat—if it had one—and squeezing. And the third... the third one damn near rips me in half as heat explodes in my balls, racing out of my cock and pumping out inside her.

"Fuck," I growl out curse after curse, gritting my teeth as my vision blurs.

I squeeze my eyes shut to maintain my balance.

"Fuck," I repeat again, opening my eyes straight into Shona's gaze.

She's panting, her eyes bright, her hair wild, sweat glistening in the channel between her breasts.

Fucking stunning.

"I think you succeeded," she gasps.

"In?"

"Making me yours for the night." Her lips curl up into a smile.

I drop to my elbows, allowing her legs to relax. But I keep myself firmly planted deep inside her as I dust my knuckles over her cheekbone.

The copper in her eyes glows like a fire on a winter's night as she looks into my eyes.

Calming. Warming. Welcoming.

I shift to get more comfortable, causing my cock to move inside her. Heat swells in my chest as she lets out a soft moan and wraps her arms around my neck, pulling me close.

I kiss her with all the tenderness a moment like this deserves.

A moment I know I could search for a lifetime to replicate, and none would stand a hope in hell of coming close.

She's unique.

Totally and utterly unique.

I pause the kiss long enough to utter my next words, a promise to her.

"Darling, I've barely begun."

Chapter 8
Shona

THE SOUND OF THE shower wakes me.

My eyes flutter open slowly, and I stretch happily against the plush, soft bedding, my spine straightening in delight. I can't recall sleeping this well in ages. When *he* finally let me sleep, that is.

Trent Forde, the most in-demand man in Hollywood, special effects master, giant cock wielder, and champion pussy eater. I've never felt so sore but sexually satisfied in my entire thirty years.

Sure, I thought something may happen when I accepted his dinner invitation. Maybe a kiss goodnight. But I didn't expect to be waking up in his giant bed, my thighs feeling like I spent a week riding the prized rodeo bull.

Oh my god.

I throw my arm over my eyes with a suppressed laugh.

Gloria was right. She said she bet he had a giant cock, and that he fucked like a... well, whatever she almost said he fucked like, she's right. Perhaps she was going to say demi-god. That's it, Trent Forde fucks like a sexual demi-god. Part man, part... fuck-machine.

He didn't stop until the early hours. We could have hooked ourselves up to LA's power grid. His energy could keep the entire city lit up.

The shower turns off and a wet Trent with a white towel wrapped around his tanned hips, and one around his shoulders, walks in and straight over to the bed, leaning to kiss me.

He smells like citrus bodywash and mint.

The best wake-up call.

"Good morning." Water droplets run down his sculpted pecs as I prop myself up on my elbows, the sheet covering my breasts.

"Morning."

He straightens, toweling his thick, dark hair, as his rich brown eyes hold mine.

"Just so you know, you're a beautiful sleeper."

I bite my lip.

Just weeks ago, I thought he was the biggest jerk to work with. But now? After spending more time with him, I can see there is so much more to him. Trent may be intense and abrasive on set. But underneath it all is a man with a passionate heart, who's had it burned. A man who cares about other people, getting them new lamps when they need them, talking fondly of his housekeeper with memory issues... plus all those photographs on his table. All filled with genuine smiles, brimming with the real happiness that being in his company does to you once he lets you get close.

I understand it. I have a matching one on my face right now.

I narrow my eyes at him playfully.

"And just so you know, I hear your compliment, and I accept it. Thank you."

He chuckles, throwing the towel onto a chair and pulling on a white t-shirt. He dresses in a pair of dark jeans, then runs his fingers through his damp hair, somehow making it look sexily styled to perfection with zero effort.

"I hate to do this, but I've got to go out. Something came up."

He sits on the bed next to me and lifts my hand, holding it to his cheek and kissing my wrist.

The swarm of butterflies from last night return once more, reporting for duty.

"Have a shower. I left clean towels out for you. And there's fresh coffee beans for the machine in the cupboard next to the wine cooler." He frowns. "I'm sorry, I don't know how long it will take."

"It's okay." I trace the lines at the corners of his eye. Smile lines.

I've got you figured out, Trent Forde.

You've only been a grumpy asshole since Claudia broke your heart.

Before that, you smiled. Really smiled. Like in the photographs downstairs. The evidence is right here on your handsome face.

His shoulders relax, and he kisses my wrist again.

"I'll call you."

Then he stands and leaves the room without looking back.

I lie back against the giant, soft pillows, and blow out a breath, looking around at his luxury bedroom, all decorated in white and muted creams, which is now empty, except for me.

The front door slams, followed by the rev of a car engine a few moments later.

Something gnaws at my stomach, and I sit upright in bed. My eyes land on my discarded clothes that Trent's folded and placed on the bottom of the bed, ready for me to put back on.

Put back on and leave.

I swallow the sudden ache in my throat.

He didn't ask for my number.

"How was your weekend?" Gloria asks as we set up our kits. We're filming the season trailer today, so everyone is here.

"It was… Yeah, it was okay."

"Did you have fun at the party? Told you he'd have an amazing house. No red room though, from what I could tell." Gloria laughs as Ralph walks in with two steaming cups. She puts her hands in a prayer position before rushing over and kissing him on both cheeks. "If you hadn't been happily married for thirty years, Ralph, then I would drive you to Vegas tonight and marry you myself. Only the best men know how to make a proper coffee." She takes a sip from her cup, moaning in appreciation. I accept mine from him with a smile.

I wrap my hand around the hot cardboard and drink, savoring it. Gloria's right. Ralph's coffee is the best. Trent's... well, I didn't stay long enough to discover what kind of coffee his state of the art, shiny machine made.

I showered when I got home. It felt odd being in his house alone after he left. There was no point staying. He said he'd call, but he never took my number, so it's hardly a surprise that my phone has been silent.

And that's fine with me.

I mean, it's an asshole thing to do when all his actions leading to that point gave different signals. He even stroked my hair and kissed my forehead as I fell asleep lying on his chest, exhausted.

But none of that matters now.

I got a night of great sex out of it.

And thinking back to what he said about missing Claudia, it's obvious now.

I was a filler fuck.

Someone you fuck while you're still getting over your ex, but not ready to move on. Or, even more likely, when you're still in love with your ex-fiancée and are trying to convince yourself you aren't, by fucking someone else.

All night long.

All night with what felt like triple figure orgasms, and a near out of body experience from the sheer strength of a certain one, which occurred while he sat against the headboard as I straddled him. He gripped my hip with one hand like his life depended upon it, dark eyes blazing into mine, the other hand curled around my throat.

Yes, Trent Forde knows how to filler fuck.

He probably invented it.

"Let's get this show on the road then." Gloria's eyes light up as Ralph heads out and Jay and another one of the male cast, dressed in SWAT costume, enter. "Come on, boys." She pats her chair, winking. "We'll take you both together."

Two hours later, she and I are standing on the side-lines as the trailer filming begins. It's quiet on set. There are multiple special effects shots to get, explosions, gun fire, fireballs; you name it. So everyone has fallen silent as Trent talks to his assistant, and then has a group discussion with the four camera operators.

He hasn't looked in my direction once.

He's in full director mode; his ball cap pulled down to shield his eyes from the morning Californian sun as he points at things on set and then checks the angle from his viewing screen. He has a director's chair, but he rarely uses it. He's an active director, striding about the set, talking to the actors, discussing the script, constantly making amendments, improvements. It's part of what makes him so brilliant.

"I love seeing a man hard at work, don't you?" Gloria crosses her arms, and I follow her line of sight to where Trent is bent over adjusting cabling, his strong thighs and ass snugly encased in his faded jeans.

"Mm." I look away.

We spend the next hour watching filming, then get back to work on makeup touch-ups and adding pretend blast soot to Jay and the other cast members' faces before they head off to film again.

By the time the end of the day rolls in, we've spent most of the day on our feet and I'm happy to hear Trent has called it a wrap. I haven't seen him again since this morning.

"Ivy, here we come," Gloria says as I pack the last of my brushes away in my kit.

"Really?" I look at her. "My feet are killing me. Don't you fancy takeout?"

She eyes me, hands on her hips. It's a tradition we started when we worked on our set together. At the end of filming each season, we go for a blowout meal at The Ivy in West Hollywood together. It's a reward for the weeks or even months of intense work we've just done.

I look forward to it, we both do.

But today, I feel... flat, deflated.

"Do not"—Gloria points a bright pink nail at me—"flake out on me. We always do this. We've earned it. Besides, it's your turn to pay."

I rub my temples and smile. She's right. It is my turn, and my somber mood is partly due to a certain silent director, who I shouldn't be letting get to me. It's not like he's the first one-night stand I've ever had.

"Okay." I throw my hands up. "Let me go get my bag from the car. I brought a change of clothes."

Gloria holds her own garment bag in the air, waving it with a grin. "Go, Doll. I'll see you in a minute."

I step out of our trailer and walk to my car, grabbing my bag from the trunk and placing my dress bag over my arm.

"Shona!"

I turn as Trent appears, cap still on, dark hair curling at the top of his navy-blue t-shirt.

"I was hoping I'd catch you." He smiles.

I simply stare at him, waiting.

His eyes pinch at the corners, his smile faltering as he studies my face.

"Are you okay?"

"I'm fine."

"Listen." He takes his cap off and runs his hand through his thick, dark, waves.

I swallow as I remember what they felt like threaded between my fingers.... and against my thighs.

"Things have been..." He places his cap back on and presses a finger and thumb into his eye sockets. "Fuck... things have been—"

"It's okay. You don't need to explain."

A small voice chants *filler fuck* in my head.

His brows pop up. "I thought you'd be pissed. I haven't called when I said I would. I just—"

"It's fine. I get it." I lift a shoulder. "We work together. It was one night. And now it's in the past."

His jaw clenches and he draws his shoulders back. "Right."

"Congratulations, by the way. What I saw filmed today looked fantastic. It's going to be amazing, as always." I turn before he can see the heat that's burning through my chest and up my neck.

A filler fuck.

I don't care. I. Do. Not. Care.

But if I'd read the signals better—his stupidly mixed ones—then I wouldn't have been so honest with him that night. I don't hide my past about my stepdad abusing my mom. It's part of my story and why I developed a love for makeup. But I went further, telling him things I wouldn't have shared if I'd known it was only a one-night thing.

I had my head on his chest, listening to his heartbeat when I confessed that even though it's been years and I may seem like a strong person, I still have dreams. Nightmares. Ones where Keith finds me. Comes back for revenge. Beats me to within an inch of my life... or worse.

I told Trent I get paranoid and think I see him from the corner of my eye. It's never him. It's just bad memories playing into my consciousness. Usually when I'm tired or have been overdoing it.

Nothing more.

I just wish I hadn't told Trent Forde all of that.

Exposed my weakness.

"Shona," he calls after me.

I turn back. His phone vibrates in his pocket. He pulls it out, glancing at the screen and then back at me.

"I'm sorry, I have to take this."

Maybe he looks apologetic, like his voice sounds; I don't know.
I'm already walking away.

Chapter 9
Shona

"MM, THIS IS TO die for." Gloria's eyes flutter closed as she moans in appreciation over her last forkful of dessert.

I admit; coming to The Ivy was a great idea. We've eaten, drank, talked, and laughed. Like we do every time as part of our tradition. Having a friend like Gloria is what someone needs when they've been blown off by a bigshot director with a giant G-spot hitting dick.

I drain the last of my champagne.

Trent Forde has not been on my mind this entire meal. I won't let him slink his way into my thoughts now.

"Shona, look."

Gloria tips her head to her right, her eyes widening as she gives me a look that means, *I've seen something scandalous and I'm holding in a squeal.*

I look around, the reason for her reaction becoming clear, three tables away.

"I can't believe they just flaunt it around so brazenly." Gloria snorts in disgust.

I swallow the surge of bile that hits my throat as I stare across the room at our dining companions.

Claudia flicks her long blonde hair over her shoulder and fawns over Ewan.

"This is LA. Shit happens all the time. They're old news," I mutter.

But that's not true.

They aren't old news to Trent.

Their deceit still affects him.

Gloria subtly turns to look again. Claudia is giggling now, her ass almost visible as her tight minidress rides up and she leans over the table to kiss Ewan on the mouth.

"He's sexy in a down and dirty way... the shaved head... I get it," Gloria says. "But he's not a patch on Trent." She screws up her nose as the sounds of their wet lips smacking together drifts across the room. "And I bet Trent doesn't sound like that when he kisses."

"No, he doesn't," I murmur.

Claudia's hands have disappeared beneath the tablecloth. I turn away after she passes Ewan a scrunched-up ball of lacy fabric.

Gloria's eyes widen.

"I know," I whisper in agreement. "Talk about obvious. The whole restaurant just saw her hand him her panties."

"No, no, no." Gloria holds up a hand. "Forget Miss Screw-your-friend-behind-your-back over there. Rewind."

"What?"

"Rewind to the part where you slipped that you have knowledge over Trent Forde's kissing style."

My brain scrabbles around for an answer.

"It was just a guess." I cross my arms and look for a server. I need some water.

"Shona. We tell the truth, you and me." She looks at me and the back of my neck grows hot.

She's right. We do. Ever since that night she drove me and Mom to hospital—the night Josh got arrested, and then released without charge—we've never had secrets. She made me promise, because she wanted to help if Keith ever came back or tried to make contact again. He hasn't, though. And we moved soon after. Mom wanted a fresh start, although she was also scared of him returning. She's much happier where she is now. It's a good neighborhood, and she has nice friends. Gloria moved, too. She often asks about Mom. Mom found the idea of staying in touch with anyone from her past too hard. Like the bad memories of anything or anyone other than me and Josh who connected to that time were too strong.

"Okay." I sit in my chair and force myself not to look in Claudia and Ewan's direction again.

The server spares me a moment longer as he comes to settle the bill. I take out my purse to pay and Gloria's eyes burn into me the entire time.

He leaves and we head to the restroom together. She takes my hand to pull me along faster.

"So, come on then." She places her purse on the counter and turns the moment we're inside.

"I ran into him at the party."

She raises her brows.

"We kissed."

She clears her throat.

"Okay, fine," I sigh. "We kissed and it was like all the movie ones we've seen filmed, only better, because it was real. And then he invited me to dinner the next night, and I went."

"Just dinner?"

My shoulders dip, and I lower my voice in case any of the stalls are occupied.

"No, not just dinner. Dinner and a night of pantie-exploding sex, okay? Like…" I side-eye her and fail to keep the quirk from the corners of my lips at her mouth hanging open. "Like, the best sex you can imagine, times a million… At least."

I put my lip gloss on and drop it back inside my purse.

"Careful. Your face might stay like that."

She jabs my upper arm.

"You're telling me this two days later?"

"We've been busy. Set was manic today."

Gloria tuts at me. That excuse won't fly, and I know it.

I turn to her. "I don't see it turning into anything. It was just a one-off."

She shakes her head.

"What's that for?"

"Doll, you don't take a man like Trent Forde for a spin for only one night. I've seen the way he looks at you. You need to lock that man down. You'd be good for the grumpy bastard." She laughs. "I thought he was in an unusually pleasant mood today. Figures if he had you keeping him company this weekend."

"Yeah, well, don't get used to it if he stays on for next season as director. There won't be a re-run," I huff.

"We'll see." Gloria smiles.

We finish in the restrooms, then walk through the restaurant and outside into the LA air.

"Damn it, I forgot I need to pick up some leather polish. Do you mind?"

"Not at all. Go ahead, I'll wait here," I say to Gloria.

I peer in at the designer purses in the window as she heads inside the store.

"Trent brought me here for my last birthday."

I turn to the voice and my stomach knots as Claudia stands next to me, a quilted Chanel purse draped over her shoulder.

"We haven't met. I'm Claudia," she says as I stare at her.

"I know who you are."

You were on the front page of every celeb magazine when you were caught out. Cheat!

"Oh." She smiles as though my admission pertains to some warped level of fame she probably thinks she has. Gloria told me once that the on-set rumor mill was that she wants to be an actress and was only dating Trent for his connections.

"And you're Trent's..."

She straightens her purse and flicks her hair as she waits for me to answer.

"Colleague. I'm his colleague."

"Oh? On *Steel Force*?" She grins. "I love that show!" She giggles.

"That's right," I answer, scanning the street over her shoulder.

Where did Ewan go?

"It didn't sound like you're just his colleague in the restroom back there." Claudia's giggle subsides, and she studies me with focused eyes.

Now, I get it. The hair, the makeup, the entire demeanor. Claudia may look like a Barbie doll, but her head isn't just air-filled plastic. She's smarter than she portrays. And it works for her; climbing the social ladder like she's doing. It's a sad fact that a lot of men feel intimidated by an intelligent woman. Especially in this town. They'd rather have arm candy to massage their ego.

"No. Definitely a colleague." I give her a tight smile as a sleek Maserati pulls up next to us.

"Well, a little girl-to-girl advice." Her eyes flick from the car back to mine. "I know this town thinks I'm the bitch who cheated on Trent. But I did love him."

I swallow the lump in my throat at the genuine sincerity in her voice.

"And there's only so much a girl can take. Trent... he works, all the time. It's why he's so successful. But be prepared to come second. No one will ever be that man's priority. Not unless you're a strobe light, or some new piece of technology." She shakes her head with a small sigh and looks back to the car where Ewan has rolled the window down and is looking over at us. "I wanted someone to fight for me." She smiles and waves at Ewan who winks at her. "Turns out, I found him. I'm just sorry it happened the way it did."

She walks over to the car before calling back, "Take care...?"

"Shona," I reply, returning her wave as she smiles and sinks into the car.

"Was that—?" Gloria exits the store and takes my arm in hers as we walk.

"It was." I purse my lips as Claudia's words run through my head.

"What did the cheating hussy want?"

"To tell me dating Trent is lonely and he didn't fight for her."

"Well, that's ridiculous." Gloria scoffs. "Honestly, cheaters always have an excuse, trying to pass the buck. It's never their fault, always someone else to blame."

"Yeah," I agree half-heartedly.

Gloria's right. In my eyes, there is no excuse for cheating. Just end one relationship before beginning another if you aren't happy.

Yet, Claudia's *girl-to-girl* advice echoes in my ears the whole way home, until all I can hear on repeat in my brain is, *No one will ever be that man's priority.*

She's right.

I've had a lucky escape.

Chapter 10
Trent

I PLACE THE PHOTOGRAPH of me, Ewan, and Claudia back inside the drawer. My head may as well be in a vise for the pounding headache I have. That's what two nights in a row of hospital lighting does to you.

I walk into the kitchen and flick the coffee machine on, then sit at the counter and drop my head into my hands.

What a headfuck couple of days.

I exhale, dragging my hands down my face, as Mom's words bring a smile to my face. Even when she's in the hospital, she's still bossing me about.

"I want to see you happy before I die."

She's so melodramatic—makes sense seeing as she was an actor before she retired. She is nowhere near dying as I've told her many times. Although, getting a call from her neighbor that she'd fallen on the front porch had my heart plummeting into my feet.

What if she'd been inside? Alone?

I knew this decision was coming, but this has cemented it for me. She'll kick up a fuss, of course. The crew might call me 'Sparky,' but that's because they haven't met my mother. If they had, then that name would be hers.

I groan and rub my stinging eyes. I've slept a grand total of six hours since Saturday due to the call Sunday morning, followed by Mom's fall. But the loss of sleep Saturday night for Shona is not something I regret in the slightest. I felt energized Sunday morning. It's like she gave me more *life*.

"You need a woman who challenges you. She needs to be able to stand up to you. I know what you can be like."

Jesus, it's like Mom's in the room. I chuckle and go to the coffee machine.

She's right, though. Whatever that bullshit Shona was trying to blow me off with about us only being for one night is just that—bullshit. She can't think that night would happen and that'd be it.

I make an espresso, then throw it straight back and grab my cell.

"Sam? You remember the way to Miss West's house, don't you?"

"Trent?"

Shona's brow wrinkles as she takes me in.

"Can I come in?"

"Sure."

She steps aside and I squeeze past her. The scent of flowers fill my lungs as I breathe her in.

"What are you—?"

Just as she closes the door, I steal the words from her mouth as I step into her so she has to lift her chin to look at me. I stretch my fingers out by my sides to relieve the tingling in them as I ache to touch her.

"Tell me, Shona. At what point on Saturday night, or Sunday morning, did I give you the idea that I didn't want more with you?"

She glares at me.

Fuck, this isn't how I had planned my opening line to go. Tiredness and irritation that she was so eager to write us off combine in a heady mixture, summoning that abrasive 'sparkiness' I'm famous for to the surface. I was going to be apologetic, explain calmly what's happened since Sunday morning.

But then I saw her.

And now she's standing right in front of me, looking at me with that fire in her eyes, and...Wham! Just like that, any sense of control is gone.

"Nice to see you too," she snaps back, crossing her arms over her chest.

Energy races around my body, spiking my heartrate as I indulge myself in a hungry assessment of her. Her eyes are narrowed and trained on mine, her lips pink, not a sign of the red lipstick she wore that first time we kissed, and her long hair flows over her shoulders, all the way down over her incredible breasts.

Breasts I fucked Saturday night before she sucked me off.

That entire night has burned itself into my brain as a core memory.

She squares up to me, the copper in her eyes igniting like I've introduced more oxygen to an internal fire raging inside her.

"You said, *be mine tonight*. Those were your words."

I lean closer.

"Maybe I should re-phrase. I meant, *be fucking mine*. Period."

The copper ring flares as she huffs out a breath.

"If this is an apology, then you're going about it in an asshole way. Next time, try sending flowers if you want me to entertain your selfishness."

I step closer so I'm toe to toe with her. She doesn't flinch. Her jaw clenches in defiance as she holds my gaze.

"I can do that. I can send fucking flowers and tell you I haven't been able to stop thinking about you, despite the fact I haven't stayed still long enough since Sunday morning for my head to stop spinning like a fucking teacup at Disneyland."

I lower my voice, trying to rein back my intensity that amps up when she looks at me like this, all pouty lips and attitude that I want to fuck out of her.

"I should have called. I'm sorry."

The pulse flutters in her neck, and I clench my hand into a fist to prevent reaching up to stroke it.

"You don't need to apologize. It was a one-time thing," she replies, flippantly, not a hint of disappointment in her voice.

And like that, I'm amped back up.

"No."

One-time thing... said so matter-of-factly, as though she doesn't give a shit. When I know the way we were with one another on Saturday night is not the behavior of two people who do *not give a shit.* You don't confess your fears after spending hours wrapped up in one another if you're never planning on spending time together again.

At least, I don't.

I slam my hand against the solid wood of the door behind her.

Her eyes widen, but she still doesn't speak, doesn't give me anything back.

She doesn't want to engage? That's fine. It'll make it easier to say what she needs to hear. I'm done with not acting on my feelings. Look where it's gotten me in the past. I'm going to say what I came to, and if she doesn't want to know, then... then, I'll fuck off and never bother her again.

She pulls her shoulders back as she stares at me, the angry energy radiating from her body in waves.

"Jesus, Shona. I'm here telling you I'm fucking crazy about you! You want to know why I didn't call and tell you that sooner? It's because I had a call from another set director Sunday morning. One of their stunts went wrong. A guy ended up in the hospital. It wasn't my company, but they wanted me to go and check everything was safe. I left a team there to take over. And when I came back home that afternoon, I got a call from Mom's neighbor saying she had a fall and was in the hospital. I spent the rest of the day and night there, and then figured I'd see you Monday and explain. Only, you blew me off. And then I was back at the hospital with Mom all night until they discharged her this morning."

I'm panting as I finish.

Shona's eyes soften as she searches mine.

"Your mom?"

"She's going to be fine."

"And the stunt guy?"

"Also fine."

Her shoulders dip, and the fire in her eyes mutes to a glowing haze.

"How much?" she whispers.

"Pardon?" I screw my face up, confused.

"How much?" she repeats, eyeing me coolly.

What's she going on about? I'm here, raging and panting like some rabid wild animal, spilling my feelings out to her, and she's what? Asking about medical bills?

"How much, Trent?" she asks a third time.

I stare back in bewilderment.

She tips her chin as she spells out each word, her eyes glued to mine.

"How fucking crazy about me are you? Is it just fucking crazy? Or is it, really, *damn, you-could lose-your-head-any-second* fucking crazy?"

The corners of my mouth twitch.

This woman.

I lean a little closer until our lips graze. Then I whisper, "Really *damn, could-lose-my-head-any-*second and *it-could-also-explode* fucking crazy. With some extra mad as shit, deranged jerk tendencies thrown in for good measure."

A faint smile settles across her lips.

"You forgot bossy-as-hell bosshole vibes."

She's so close I can taste her breath on the tip of my tongue.

"I really want to kiss you right now." My lips brush hers with each word. "I don't know what's gotten into me since you slapped me with your attitude on the set, Shona West. But I'm a sucker for it."

My heart pounds as she looks at me from under her lashes.

"If you want to do it so bad, then what's stopping you." Her voice is breathy, the way it sounded Saturday night when she was turned on. Her breasts press against my chest as she leans closer.

It would be so easy to lose myself in her this second.

But I can't. Not when I still need to say the most important thing she needs to hear. Because if we are to stand any hope, then she must know what I value above anything else. I will never accept another Claudia situation in my life ever again.

"You are," I state. "You're stopping me. You're so eager to write me off over a misunderstanding and some miscommunication. I'm telling you, Darling. I want you. I want everything to do with you. And I'll give you the same in return. But you *will* trust me. Without trust, we have nothing."

She draws in a slow breath.

"Trust," I repeat. "I'll give you mine if you give me yours."

"You've had yours abused, Trent. I get it."

I breathe deeply, my chest rising and falling, and watch her.

A crease appears between her eyebrows. "You don't want Claudia back?"

"Fuck no! Why the hell would you think that?"

Her gaze drops to my lips and back up. "You said you missed one more than the other."

Memories of their deceit roll through me, twisting my gut. "Ewan. I meant, Ewan. He was my friend. His betrayal was a million times worse."

Shona stays firmly planted with her back against the door, caged in on one side by my arm, free on her other side.

She could move away if she wanted to. She could leave. Tell me to get out.

But she doesn't.

She stands and assesses me with those damn entrancing copper rings glowing in her eyes. Telling me without words I need to take a chance on her. If Claudia and Ewan's lies have taught me anything, it's that I still want to have someone I can trust. I still want that. I won't let them take any more away from me.

This is my life. And how I choose to live it is my fucking choice and no one else's.

"You know what I'm a sucker for, Mr. Forde?" Shona echoes my earlier words.

My dick twitches in my pants at the way my name rolls off her tongue.

"Tell me," I urge, holding in my groan as she licks her lips.

"It's when you boss me around and think that means you're the one in control."

I reach up and curl my fingers around her neck, relishing in the way her eyes darken with lust as I stroke her jaw with my thumb.

"Trust me, Darling. I know you have all the power. I wouldn't have it any other way."

"You're a complicated bastard." The corners of her mouth lift. "And you know what?"

"What?" I murmur, captivated by the way her lips are moving as she speaks.

She bites the plump bottom one before answering.

"I wouldn't have you any other way either. In fact, I *trust* you to never change. I like you exactly the way you are. Confident. Brilliant. Passionate."

"Crazy about you?" I arch a brow, and she smirks, giving me a small nod.

It's all the invitation I need to push forward and drive my tongue inside her mouth, kissing her with an urgency that she matches as her hands sink into my hair.

"You're harder to handle than the most unstable explosives we can legally have on set," I grumble as I sink into her.

She laughs and pulls me against her, positioning her legs either side of my thighs. She grinds shamelessly against the denim, whimpering, the vibrations of which reverberate through my palm on her neck.

"Trying to make a mess on my jeans, Darling?"

"I'm merely trying to entertain myself while I wait for you to fuck me. It counts as a make-up one. So it should be fast and hard."

Jesus.

I slip a hand underneath her dress, stifling a groan, as my fingers slip straight inside her soaked panties.

She drops her hands to my pants and undoes them.

"Is that right?" I murmur.

She gasps against my lips as I sink two fingers inside her wet heat and run my thumb around her swollen clit, pinning her to the wall and fingering her deep enough that her toes dance against the floor.

"Trent..."

I suck in a sharp breath as she calls my name at the same time as freeing my throbbing cock from my pants and stroking it up and down.

"Yes?" I grit, heat spreading over the back of my neck as she reaches the tip of my cock and rubs my precum over it with the pad of her thumb.

"Hurry up and put a condom on. I want to come with you inside me."

Arousal blurs my vision as I grab a condom from the wallet in the back pocket of my jeans and tear the wrapper.

I take a deep breath. I need to see straight. I need to be inside her.

We need to *make up*.

I need this woman in my life. She was unplanned. Ever since that day on set she took the role and delivered those lines perfectly, something inside me knew. It's as if life was sending me a great big fucking clue, gift-wrapped in a bow.

Everything about Shona screams challenge. She will test my fucking resolve. I know it.

And I will welcome it every single day.

With open fucking arms.

"Let me."

She takes the condom from my hands and rolls it down onto me as I groan, my balls pulling up to my body.

"Fast and hard?" I arch a brow at her once she has me wrapped.

"Fast and hard."

I grab her thighs and lift, pressing her to the wall and holding her so she's poised on the sensitive tip of my cock.

"Watch as I pull you down and fill every inch of your cunt, Darling."

Her breath stalls, a flush creeping up her neck as she drops her gaze to where our bodies meet.

Then I drag her slowly onto my raging erection, moaning a deep curse, as she wraps around me like she was made to fit me, and only me.

"Now watch me," I growl, as I lift her and slam back inside.

Her eyes return to mine, and the intensity between us is palpable as I thrust up into her repeatedly. I swear I can almost touch our arousal and desire for one another. It's hanging in the space between us as I drive into her, our bodies chasing an all-consuming high together. It's thick in the air, but not like smoke, choking and toxic; it's like oxygen, feeding the fire in her eyes when she looks at me, feeding the fire in my heart when I look at her.

Feeding every damn fiber in my body as my balls tingle and the length of my cock throbs with the need to come inside her.

"I'm going to fill this pretty pussy any second. Tell me you're—"

"God!" Shona cries out, her nails digging into my shoulders as she spasms around me. "I'm coming!"

Her going off like a rocket is too much to handle. My orgasm bursts from me as her body wrings my cock dry. The sensation that each pulse of her body creates around me draws spurt after spurt of release from me at breakneck speed.

"Fuck!" I sink my head into the crook of her neck, burying my nose in her hair as I continue to come. "You're incredible, You're..." She squeezes around me, coming a second time, crying out my name.

I press my lips to hers, swallowing her moans as she shudders and keeps coming around me in waves.

"Incredible... so fucking unique," I utter, kissing her over and over until she's spent in my arms.

"Your bed is nice. I could live here." I press my nose to the pillow, inhaling her floral scent and tightening my arms around her from behind.

"How would you get any work done?" She shuffles deeper into my arms, turning her face to the side, so she can kiss me over the top of her shoulder.

"Who needs work?" I kiss from her mouth, down the side of her neck and across her shoulder.

"Maybe it's true what they say about men's brains being in their dicks. You must have fired yours all out with the sex, because the Trent Forde I know would never say that about work."

I chuckle, resuming my exploration of her skin.

"True. I love what I do. But I don't want to only have one love for the rest of my life."

She stiffens in my arms.

Too far, Trent. This is date two, and it's not even a date. It's make-up sex after screwing up date one spectacularly.

"You want it all, huh? Knew you were selfish."

She giggles as I pull her back against me, tickling her and attacking her neck with my mouth.

"When it comes to you, I do. I want everything. Starting with another orgasm on my face."

"Three not enough for you?" Shona fires back, her voice laced with playfulness.

We spent the evening in bed together, 'making up,' and then I slept like a fucking log in her bed with her curled around me.

Best. Night. Ever.

"Don't you have meetings today? I know set's closed for the end of season break. But don't you have other projects you're working on?" She sinks back against me as I run my nose up the side of her face and kiss her temple.

"I do. But today's are all rescheduled."

"Oh. To be with your mom?"

"I want to check on her, yes. But she has a nurse staying with her at her house for a few days. I want to spend my day with you."

She turns in my arms.

"You haven't used your phone since you got here."

"No, I haven't."

Her eyes narrow. "Trent Forde, did you change your meetings for me before you even knew if I was going to be home? Before you even knew if we would be talking again?"

"I'd have sat on the step outside until you came home if you weren't in."

"What about if I'd brought another man home?"

I stiffen at the mere mention of another man being in Shona's immediate vicinity. Let alone coming into her home.

"I'd have had to break his nose. Then break every finger so he couldn't touch you."

The copper in her eyes glows, and I study the way it looks like dancing flames as her pupils dilate.

"You wouldn't."

"Try me, Darling. I promise you if another man had his hands on you, then he'd be lucky to survive." I catch her bottom lip between my teeth. "You're mine now. Period. Remember?"

"Of course. The period makes it official."

"Damn straight."

She lets out a soft laugh, wrapping her arms around my neck. I kiss her until we're both rocking up against each other with increased desperation.

"Now get yourself up here and sit," I growl. "It's time for number four."

Chapter 11
Shona

"Made them extra hot for you today, ladies. Going to be another busy day."

"Thanks, Ralph!" Gloria and I call as he exits our trailer with a wave.

We've had a few weeks working on smaller projects while season filming took a break. But now we're back on set for a week, filming a special collaboration episode of *Steel Force*. The show's producers joined forces with a legal drama that takes place between both LA and New York to film a joint episode. The result being a set buzzing with activity and twice as many cast and crew members as usual.

"How does Trent feel about having another director to work with today?" Gloria asks as we set up our kits.

"You know, I think he's been looking forward to it. It means he can loosen the reins just a little and concentrate on the effects they've planned."

He's been so animated telling me about his plans for this episode. He's going all out with the special effects. We've got high speed car chases planned, a shipping dock fire with multiple explosions, and underwater filming with a submerged tank with someone locked inside as it sinks.

Basically, my man is in his element.

It's been three and a half blissful weeks since he came to my place and laid his feelings bare for me. Threw them all out into the open.

Unapologetic. Direct. In control.

Trent Forde in full pantie-melting mode.

I love it. I love how he doesn't want to play games. If he wants something, he goes for it. If he thinks something needs saying, he says it. If he wants something done, it's done. Straight away. No messing around.

It's the best relationship I've ever had. It's early days, but so far, Trent has turned my life upside down in the best way possible. And the sex…

"You've got that smug look on your face again." Gloria's shoulders vibrate as she laughs. "I would have too if I was dating my own Sparky."

His nickname used to be heard around set for all the wrong reasons. He's maintained his respect and his brilliance, but there's something else that's creeped its way onto the set this last month.

Fun.

The crew's laughing and smiling more.

There's a lighter energy. The set ran well before because Trent was on top of everything. But now it's better. There's an excited buzz in the air. And his nickname doesn't elicit the subtle eye rolls, or the 'he's brilliant, but…' comments. Now it's a badge of honor. 'Sparky' echoes around set like a mantra, lifting spirits, motivating us on early morning starts. Basically, bringing us together as one giant team with the same goal of creating something special.

And Trent feels the shift too.

He's smiling more every day. It's become more natural to him than his previous glary-eyed mask of concentration.

Gloria hums as we continue working.

"Aren't you glad you didn't listen to what his ex said?"

"Ugh, Claudia."

Why she felt she needed to warn me, I don't understand. Maybe she thought she was helping, saying I'd never be a priority to Trent. But she was wrong. Perhaps he has always put work first in the past. But he's only prioritized our relationship since that day he came to my house. He's stopped meetings running over when he's told me he'll take me for dinner, so that he's never late. He even shifted an entire day's filming schedule around to look after me when I caught a one-day sickness bug.

Trent Forde is incredible.

"Saying he wouldn't fight for you. Complete bullshit," Gloria continues.

"Of course," I agree.

There's no dragon to slay to rescue me from a tower. I wouldn't want him to, even if there were. I'm a grown-ass woman, not a damsel in distress, incapable of fighting her own battles.

Him forcing the issue of trusting each other is fighting for us. He's fighting for us to have a grown-up, mature relationship, where we are open and honest with each other.

That's a fight I'm onboard with winning alongside him.

"Told you banging him would be good for everyone." Gloria cuts back into my thoughts.

Jay walks in, and Gloria steals him, inviting him straight into her chair as her face lights up like Christmas came early.

My cell beeps with a message.

Josh: Hey, Sis. I know you're busy today but call me when you can. I need to talk to you ASAP.

He's caught me in time. I have my phone on silent when I watch filming.

Trent needs all distractions to a minimum. He has to concentrate. We all do. It may be for show, but the danger is real with the equipment he works with. He loves it. But if there's a day he's going to feel stressed or be wound tighter than usual, then a full day like today will do it.

He's already told me we won't see each other tonight as he wants to personally check the set to make everything safe and take things apart.

It's going to be a late night for him, so Gloria and I have planned to hang out at my place and get a takeout.

Girls' night.

I hit dial and call Josh back.

Chapter 12
Trent

I bound up the steps to Shona's front door two at a time. I can't wait to see her face when she realizes I finished early. Set was cleared up quicker than I thought, and what we could leave safely until tomorrow to dismantle, we have.

I wanted to get here.

To have her in my arms.

To tell her what I've known for weeks already, but debated over whether it was too soon to tell her.

These past few weeks have been incredible. My mom was worried I'd have trouble letting anyone get close again. Truth be told, I was too.

Until Shona.

Shona West, my brilliant firecracker. The only woman who has ever challenged me and is happy to put me in my place again, and again.

Sometimes, I play the grump on purpose so she'll chastise me. Call me crazy, but nothing gets my dick twitching and my pulse racing like Shona when she looks like she's about to bust my balls.

I can't get enough of her.

My fist hovers mid-air by the door as a muffled moan comes from inside, followed by a man's deep laugh.

I lean close to listen.

Has someone come over?

If Shona had a male friend who she was close enough with to be visiting her at home at ten o'clock at night, then I'd already know about him. I'd already have met him. Wouldn't I?

Another moan seeps through the closed front door, followed by a rumble of a deep voice.

What the fuck is going on?

I bring my fist down against the wood in three large bangs. The door rattles in its frame, conveying my growing sense of dread.

There's another man in there with her. At fucking ten at night, when she thought I was working.

There's only one possible reason for it.

"Open up, Shona!" I yell, the muscle in my jaw aching as I grind my teeth and scan up and down the sidewalk for any vehicles I recognize.

Please, not someone I know. Not again.

The man inside laughs again. But I can't hear Shona. I can't hear anything else.

Who is this fucker? I'll have his head on a fucking spike.

"Open the fuck up, Shona!" My fist is halfway to slamming against the wood again when the door flies open.

"Who the hell are you?"

The dark-haired man who looks to be in his mid-thirties squares up to me as he fills the doorway.

"I could ask you the same fucking question!"

I barge past him, stomping straight inside.

"Shona!"

"Hey!" A large hand grabs my shoulder and yanks me back. "I don't know who the fuck you think you are, man. But you can't storm in here like this."

I turn and glare at him, a million threats communicated through my murderous expression as I snarl at him.

"She's my girlfriend, you asshole."

He snorts, his eyes widening. "Yeah, and she's my—"

"Trent?" Shona's voice rings out with shock.

I drag my gaze away from the death stare he's giving me and turn to her.

The blood in my veins runs cold.

Blood.

So much blood.

In her hair, down her t-shirt.

All over her face.

One of her eyes is swollen and bruising, and there's a deep cut on her eyebrow.

"Trent." Her good eye widens, and she holds her hands up in front of herself, glancing over my shoulder at the stranger behind me.

"Call the cops," I hiss.

I turn back to the stranger.

This has to be the asshole, Keith, who used to beat her and her mom. She was scared he'd find her. And now he has.

"Trent!" Shona yells again, but she sounds too far away, replaced by blood rushing in my ears.

She said Keith wasn't much older than her.

She said he used to laugh when he pushed her around. Pull her by her hair, throw her into the furniture and call her clumsy. Then he used to beat her mother so hard when she stood between them that he once knocked two of her teeth out.

Fucking vile excuse for a human.

His eyes widen in the split second before my fist connects with his face, blood spraying from his nose over my shirt.

But I don't let it stop me.

He's going to look like the aftermath of a meat factory after ten tons of explosives have ripped through it by the time I'm finished with him.

He falls to the floor.

Out cold.

And I throw myself on top of him, gripping him around the neck.

"Wake up, you son of a bitch! I want you to look at me when I kill you!"

"Trent!" Shona runs over and screams in my face as she pushes at me.

Then another set of hands try to pull me back. I turn to see it's Gloria. Her face is contorted with shock, and in the center of her forehead, there's a fresh gunshot wound.

The fuck?

"You should be dead." Confused, pins and needles race over my skin, covering every inch of it. "What the fuck's going on?"

A giant force crashes into me as Shona flies into me. She screams, hammering at my chest with her hands until I stumble off Keith's body and into a heap on the floor next to him.

"You just killed my brother! That's what the fuck's going on!"

"Your brother?"

Bile rises in my throat, filling my windpipe until I can't breathe.

"It's Josh, you stupid idiot! It's Josh."

Shona squeezes his shoulders, then strokes his blood-covered face. It lolls to one side, his eyes rolled back in his head.

I hit him hard. I hit him so fucking hard.

I hunch over and gag, the sound of Gloria's frantic 9-1-1 call echoing in my ears.

"Come as fast as you can. He's not waking up."

I killed him.

I killed her fucking brother.

Chapter 13
Trent

I DIDN'T KILL HIM.

But I broke his nose and gave him a concussion. He's got to stay in the hospital for a couple of days—the small snippet of information I extracted from Gloria after sitting on a hard plastic hospital chair for two hours.

"Jesus." I drop my head into my hands as she stares at me.

"I can see why you did it. She told you about Keith, didn't she?"

"Yeah."

I drag my hands down my face, then look up at the solemn expression on her face. The majority of her 'gunshot' wound has gone now. After a lady screamed in the hospital waiting area at the sight of her, Gloria went to the restroom and scrubbed off the majority of the makeup she was wearing.

They were practicing, trying out some new kit together.

I am such a fucking idiot.

Hit first, ask questions later.

All I could think at the time was that Keith had found Shona. The blood on her face, the bruising, the cut. It all looked so realistic. It all felt so goddamn sickening the second I laid eyes on her.

I told myself I'd always act on my gut in future, that I'd never ignore a feeling that something wasn't right.

I could have killed him. God knows I wanted to. The rage surging through my flesh when I thought he was Keith, when I thought he had touched Shona, *my Shona*... I...

"Lucky for you, he's going to be fine. Although I want to floor you myself for putting Shona through that. She saw her mother beaten enough. She didn't need to see her brother almost murdered in front of her."

Tension assaults my shoulders.

What have I done?

"I need to see her." I hang my head in remorse before looking up at Gloria. "To tell her how sorry I am."

She must feel bad for my pathetic pleading ass, because she gives me a half smile and tips her head to the hallway.

"She's gone to the restroom. You might catch her before she goes back in to see Josh."

"Thank you." My heart pounds as I make my way down the corridor.

I followed the ambulance to the hospital. But besides Gloria, no one will tell me anything. I'm not family so I'm not allowed any information, or to go in the room where Josh has been checked over by the doctors.

I pause, hovering in the corridor, looking at the ladies' restroom door down the hall. She'll have to walk right past me to get to Josh's room.

I wipe my sweating palms on my jeans. The backs of my knuckles are still caked in dried blood.

His blood. My girlfriend's older brother.

Fuck, I swear my heart is about to leap out of my chest.

What's she going to say? Will she even talk to me?

Her brother, for god's sake. The guy who saved her and her mom. He's the reason Shona survived and I was able to meet her, to be with her, to feel the way I do about her...

Before I can register what my feet are doing, I'm striding into the room next to me and closing the door behind me.

"Took your sweet time, jackass."

I jerk my head back as the guy in the bed addresses me, an undercurrent of warning to his tone.

"My wife's going to want your head. We've got a christening next weekend, and we're the godparents. I'm going to look great in the photos."

I cast my eyes over his swollen face. One side is twice the size of the other, a deep bruise forming around one eye.

It only makes the glare he's giving me even more menacing.

"I'm so sorry. Truly sorry. I thought you were—"

"The fucker who would have killed my sister and mom years ago if I hadn't stopped him?"

Hearing him confirm my worst fears, that Shona might not be here today, has nausea balling low in my gut and sweat breaking out along my hairline.

"Yeah." I blow out a breath, my lungs deflating.

"What would you have done if I had been him?"

"Killed you," I answer without missing a beat, fire burning in my veins as I clench my fists at the mere thought of Keith being anywhere near Shona.

Josh's steely gaze penetrates me like he's seeing right inside me, sucking out my secrets, my weaknesses, my fears.

He's big and muscular and has an air of calm authority about him. He isn't someone you want to mess with.

Unless your name is Trent Forde and you're a fucking idiot.

"Killed him because…?"

"No one touches her! No one!" I grit, pointing at Josh's face. "No one will ever fucking touch her again."

I drop my hand, squeezing my eyes shut and sucking in deep breaths to bring my sudden spike in heartrate back down.

Just one mention of Keith and I'm ready to go to war.

"All right, then."

I snap my eyes open. Josh is looking at me with an amused glint, and he's trying to smile, beneath the swelling.

"All right?"

He taps his fingers against the hospital bed sheets as he studies me.

"Shona told me about you, Trent. Said you were a great guy. That's why I dropped by to stay the night. She wanted me to meet you tomorrow. Seems you beat me to it... literally."

I stare at him. There's no mistaking the smirk forcing its way out beneath his injuries.

"I'm sorry."

His eyes never leave mine. "Listen. I'm not. I'm not sorry at all. I mean, yeah, my face is too pretty to be banged up." He chuckles. "But the fact is, you protected my sister."

"I'd do it again... under different circumstances," I add.

"I can see that."

Josh smiles this time.

I pull my brows together, not sure whether to feel immense relief, or confusion.

"So... we're good?"

"Yeah." He holds my gaze. "You keep looking out for Shona, and we're good. But you ever hurt her and—"

"I won't."

"Probably best I don't finish that sentence anyway..."

He spots something behind me, and I turn.

"Trent." Shona glares at me, her arms folded across her chest. "What the hell are you doing in here? He's supposed to be resting, he has a concussion." She looks from me to Josh and then grabs my arm and yanks me into the corridor, closing the door behind us.

"I was apologizing to your brother."

The copper rings in her eyes are in full devastation mode, burning brighter and wilder than I've ever seen.

"You have no right to be in there after what you did," she hisses, keeping her voice low as a nurse walks past.

"You don't think I'm sorry?" I counter, staring into her eyes. "Shona, I thought he was Keith. I thought he'd hurt you. You looked like you'd been beaten."

I rake my fingers through my hair, dragging in a deep breath. I'm losing my head again, as I only ever seem to do around her. She makes me crazy, impulsive. She makes me want to do ridiculous things, like almost murder a man with my bare hands.

I should apologize, beg for her forgiveness.

"I'm sorry," I try again, softening my voice. "I thought you were in danger. When I saw your face, and Josh answered the door... I'd do anything for you, Shona."

Her expression remains hard.

"You could have *killed* him."

It's better not to answer. Because had it been Keith, then I would have fucking killed him. I'm sure of it. And I can't say I would have felt even an ounce of remorse about it.

"I'm sorry."

Her shoulders drop with a deep exhale. Her face is still covered in smudges of fake blood, and I have to refrain myself from reaching up and wiping a smear from her cheek.

"Remember when you said if we don't have trust, we have nothing?" Her eyes pinch at the corners. "Where was the trust when I shouted your name? Where was the trust in giving me a split second to talk to you before you hit him? You broke his nose, Trent. What was next, every finger on his hands?"

She sighs after repeating my words about what I'd do to a man's hands if he touched her.

Because I wanted her to be mine. Period.

"I—"

"I'm sorry... I can't talk about this right now." She steps back and holds up a hand, dropping her eyes away from mine. "I'm exhausted. And... and I'm drained, okay? You should go."

"Shona—"

"Just go, Trent, please," she says wearily.

My tongue is suddenly too big in my mouth. Either that or my mouth and throat are closing up. Sweat beads on the back of my neck as she stares at me sadly.

Don't turn your back on me, Darling, please.

"I'll wait in reception. I can take you home when—"

"No." She grasps the handle to Josh's room.

"Tomorrow, then? I'll come to your place in the morning, we can—"

"Stop. Just stop."

"Shona, please?" Cold panic laces around my heart.

I've ruined everything.

"Go home, Trent," she whispers, her eyes glassy as they fill with tears.

Then she goes inside the room.

I catch a few words before the door swings shut.

"Where's Trent?" *Josh's voice.*

"Gone. He's gone."

Chapter 14
Shona

THE FOLLOWING WEEK PASSES in a blur. Trent left me a voicemail saying he'll give me space if that's what I need. But I haven't called back. I'm too confused to speak to him.

And sad.

Because despite everything, him hurting Josh, those feelings of helplessness that hit me like a truck the second he punched Josh and I was powerless to stop it—feelings that took me back to a time I would rather forget—despite all of that, I *miss* him.

I miss Trent so much that my body physically aches like I have a hole in my chest.

My phone rings and I swipe it off the kitchen side as I flick on the coffee machine.

"Hey."

"Hey, Sis. Happy Birthday!"

I smile as Josh renditions me with an overly enthusiastic song.

"Doofus."

"So, what are you doing today? Big plans?"

I sigh as I lean back against the counter.

"That great, huh?" He chuckles.

"How's your face?" I ask, already feeling lighter from hearing his voice.

"Still devilishly handsome."

I laugh as he probes in the way big brothers love to.

"You spoken to the poor fucker yet?"

"No."

"Look, it's your life, Sis. But a bit of big brotherly advice?"

"Go on, then." I snort, knowing he'll tell me anyway.

"That man will rein hell on earth for you. I felt it in his fist when it connected with my face." Josh chuckles. "Give him a break. He's probably crying into his morning coffee as we speak, hoping you'll be feeling charitable on your birthday and actually return his call."

"He doesn't know it's my birthday," I murmur as I grab a cup from the cupboard and place it beneath the coffee machine.

It's brand new, and only makes me think of Trent every morning when I use it. I admired the way his made my morning cup, so he bought me the exact same model. He told me his preference was that I drink all my morning coffees at his place, but this would do until then.

I've never dated a man so sure of everything.

Trent knows what he wants. And he doesn't try to hide it. The hurt in his voice in the voicemail he left me tells me—Trent Forde wants me back.

He wants me.

And I want him, too.

I want him more than anything. But it's been a week. How can I suddenly return his call after so long and tell him that I'm sorry I overreacted? That the memory of feeling helpless is what made me so angry, so hurt?

Him hitting Josh wasn't the problem.

The problem was me.

Trent was reacting to a situation that looked bad. He was protecting me. Josh has told me multiple times and so has Gloria.

He was *fighting* for me.

That day I saw Claudia and she said Trent Forde will never fight for anyone, she was wrong.

He fought for me, and I pushed him away and blamed him for it. And after a week of silence, he's still fighting for me by giving me the space he thinks I need.

"You going out with Gloria, then? She's always been nuts. You'll have a great time."

"Yeah." I tune back into Josh. "We're going out for lunch. Some new place she wants to try. Says it's 'out of this world' apparently."

"Well, have fun. And, Shona?"

"Yes?"

"I love you, Sis."

"I love you too."

"Why are we here?" I step out of Gloria's car in the *Steel Force* parking lot and smooth down my pale blue dress.

"I have to pick something up. It won't take a second, then we'll get straight to lunch, I swear."

"Okay. Why are there so many cars?"

I follow behind her as she swipes her ID card to grant us access. Set is deserted now that filming's finished. There should only be security patrolling it.

"Beats me."

I scan the cars quickly. No Maclaren Spider. Trent isn't here.

My heart sinks.

Do I want him to be? What would I do if I saw him? Would he even want to speak after I've ignored him for days?

This morning I listened to his voicemail again, like I have every morning since.

What if he's given up? I'd deserve it.

"Just in here." Gloria swipes the scanner to one of the giant hangars we rarely use. Last I recall, it was housing part of an old Atlantic Airways aircraft we used in an episode.

"What do you have to collect from in here?" I follow her into the pitch black.

"Hang on, the switch is here somewhere… it's…"

The space explodes into a shower of cascading stars all over the ceiling as a full planetarium roof lights up.

"Surprise!"

My step falters as more lights come on, illuminating the entire cast and crew, bunched together by the far wall underneath a giant banner that says, *Happy Birthday.*

"How the...? You did this?"

I turn to Gloria, eyes wide. She's grinning, her hands clasped as she gazes around the space. Music plays and arms embrace me as everyone comes to wish me a happy birthday.

Everyone except the only person capable of pulling this off.

"Where is he?" I ask Gloria once I've said hello to everyone and the party hits full swing. Ralph starts the dancing off by being the first on the floor.

"He said it's for you, Shona. He stayed away." She gives me a sad smile.

"But he... he did all of this."

I gaze around the space again. This must have taken him days to prepare, maybe even weeks. It's like we are in space right now. There's a set of NASA space suits that people are trying on before stepping inside a giant clear dome that's managing to create zero gravity.

My mouth drops open as someone inside floats off the ground.

"Trent did all this." I wrinkle my nose. "He doesn't even know it's my birthday."

"Oh, he knows." Gloria wraps her arm around my shoulders and squeezes. "When it comes to you, that man misses nothing."

I swallow, trying to ease the dry, scratchy lump in my throat.

He should be here.

He's done this.

He should *be* here.

"Where are you going?" Gloria calls after me as I bolt for the door, pulling my high heels off so I can run.

"Keep the party going. Make sure everyone has enough to drink. I'll be back."

"Mission accepted." Her laugh echoes in my ears, before she shouts, "Open bar!" to a loud cheer.

I run barefoot to the parking lot.

Shit! I don't have my car. Gloria drove.

"Shona, here."

I turn and hold my hands out instinctively as Jay throws his keys.

"Seriously?" I glance at his Ferrari and then back at him.

"She'll get you there in no time." His blue eyes crease at the corners. "Now go. Tell Trent to get his ass back here. He's missing all the fun."

"Thank you."

I grin as I slide into the cool interior and start the engine. It purrs to life, and I floor the accelerator.

"Trent? It's Shona." I knock harder on the door.

Maybe he didn't hear me. Or maybe he's out? Maybe I've missed him, or he knows it's me and he's ignoring the door and—

"Wonderful, you're here. It's so nice to meet you."

"Um... and you."

I don't have time to respond properly before a frail hand takes mine and leads me inside.

"I told him you'd come, Shona." The lady smiles at me sweetly. "He could never have married that hussy, Claudia." She tuts, holding my hand in hers and patting the back. "I told him he needs a woman who challenges him." Her eyes glaze over. "Do you like tea? I'll make us some." She lets go of my hand and shuffles toward the kitchen, pausing at the table of photographs and scanning over them.

She extends a shaky hand, opening the drawer, then murmuring to herself as she takes out a frame and places it on the table.

"Keeps putting it away... I don't know..." she mutters.

"Um..." I glance around the hallway, then follow her into the kitchen. "Tea sounds lovely, thank—"

My words are stolen at the sight of Trent walking in through the back door from the garden.

"Who are you talking to, Mom? Oh—"

Our eyes lock as though we haven't seen each other in years and can't quite believe the other person is real.

My heart constricts at the sight of him, all dark hair, tousled from the breeze outside, deep brown eyes brightened with hope as they hold mine.

"You left the poor girl standing on the doorstep, Trent. Where are your manners?" The sweet lady tuts as she moves over to the cupboard and busies herself getting out mugs.

Trent looks at her, then back at me, drawing in a breath.

"Shona, this is my mom, Helen."

Helen turns and smiles at me.

"Hello, Shona. I told him you would come. Do you like tea? I can make us some." She turns back to the cups and spoons sugar into them.

"Tea sounds great, Mom." Trent smiles warmly at her before walking over to me. "We'll be back in a minute. I'm just going to show Shona something."

He walks over and places his hand low on my back, ushering me out into the hallway.

I open my mouth, speaking in a hushed voice. "Your mom's sweet, she—"

"She has Alzheimer's." Trent's eyes pinch at the corners as he turns to face me. "It's been getting worse. Since her fall, I made plans for her to move in here. She has her own guest wing and a visiting caregiver, but she likes to spend time in the main house when I'm home."

Worry lines are etched into his forehead as he glances back toward the kitchen door.

My heart constricts in my chest. He's been dealing with this alone while I've been busy being mad at him. What kind of girlfriend am I?

What kind of *person* am I?

A terrible one, evidently.

"I'm so sorry," I whisper, looking between his eyes. "You never told me about her, I didn't—"

"I wanted you to meet her. And then…"

Before I screwed it all up and went mad bitch on him.

I'm sure that's what he's thinking but is too polite to say it.

"Trent," I choke.

"Don't, Shona. It's not your fault, it's mine."

I drag my eyes back to his from where I've been staring at the photograph of him, Claudia, and Ewan, that Helen placed back on the table.

"How can you say that? It *is* my fault. I didn't listen to you when you tried to explain. I pushed you away, and—"

Trent reaches to the photograph and puts it back inside the drawer.

"Not your housekeeper," I say softly.

He shakes his head with a sad smile.

"Mom gets confused. She knows a frame belongs in that space. It's not a shrine to Claudia. She never liked her, even when we were dating."

"I know. She said she's a hussy and you could never have married her."

He chuckles, some of the tension melting off his face. "She said that before she got ill as well."

I smile at him as silence falls between us.

"She's doing okay, you know. It doesn't stop her from bossing me about."

"Good. Someone needs to keep you on your toes." I bite my lip as his eyes meet mine.

Now that I'm standing here in front of his broad frame, I'm aching to touch him, my body yearning for that contact I've so dearly missed.

No-one has even touched me or held me the way Trent does.

Like I'm the most precious thing in the world.

"You're missing a great party," I add as we keep staring at one another, so many unsaid things hanging in the air.

His eyes soften. "It's for you. Not me. I should have said already, forgive me, but happy birthday."

My heart flutters in my chest.

"It would be a much happier one if you can forgive me," I whisper.

I catch the flinch of pain in his eyes before he blinks it away.

"There's nothing to forgive. I let you down. I brought back memories of a time that was painful for you. I am *so* sorry, Darling."

I suck in a breath, my heart stalling at his deep voice calling me *Darling* again.

I've missed it.

I've missed everything about him.

My voice cracks as I step closer to him.

"I should have spoken to you instead of hiding away being mad. You've had your trust broken before, and I knew that. Yet, when you needed me to listen to you, to give you a chance to explain, I shot you down and closed you out. I should have been someone you could trust not to do that to you."

"I trust you with my life, Shona. You're one of the few people I do trust."

He looks at me with such sincerity I swear my heart cries inside my chest.

"Trent..." My vision blurs as I reach for him, wrapping my arms around his neck and sinking my face into his chest.

"Hey, hey." He envelops me in his arms, rubbing my back in soothing strokes. "It's your birthday, Darling. Don't cry. Don't you ever cry over me... over us. I will be here for you no matter what. You could refuse to speak to me for a year and I'd still be here for you. A damn decade... a century."

I smile into his chest between tears, then take a deep, steadying breath.

"I'm such an idiot. I was mad at myself for being mad at you, and I didn't know what to say. I picked up my phone every day wanting to call you. I just didn't know how. I knew I'd let you down. I didn't know how to come back from where we were. From where I put us."

"We don't need to come back." Trent presses a kiss into my hair. "We only need to move forward."

"Can we do that?" I lift my chin so I can look into his eyes. "Without you, my life feels flat. There's no spark."

"No spark?"

"I need Sparky back."

His eyes light up.

"If my mother wasn't in the next room, I could show you a giant spark right here."

He grins and then grabs either side of my face between his hands, pressing his lips against mine and kissing me with a force that steals my breath and has me swirling in light-headed dizziness.

"I'm so sorry," I murmur against his lips. "I'm so sorry. I'll make it up to you, I promise. If you'll let me? If I haven't ruined us too much."

"Don't." He kisses my words away, sliding his tongue between my lips as he pulls me close to him. "You'll always have me."

He rests his forehead against mine.

"You have every part of me, Shona. *Every* part."

"You still want me to be yours?" I pull back to search his eyes, needing to see his answer, needing to feel it in his arms, to hear it in his voice.

"I always want you to be mine. Period. Great big, obvious as you can possibly make it... Period."

I tighten my arms around him.

"Trent?"

He searches my eyes.

"I want that too."

Chapter 15
Shona

"I can't believe you did all this in secret." I lie back on the cushions and blanket next to Trent.

"Do you like it?"

"I do." I gaze at the planetarium roof filled with sparkling stars.

We've had an incredible afternoon of fun, laughter, and dancing with our friends. Helen came back to the party with us. She had a great time dancing with Ralph and meeting Gloria, Jay, and the rest of the team. Sam came to collect her as the party ended and took her home where her caregiver was waiting to help out. She put up quite a fight about leaving. Told Sam he would have to drag her dead body out if he tried to make her leave before she had finished her dance with Jay.

She's incredible and not afraid to speak her mind.

Now I know why Trent says he admires my strength. He's been raised by a strong woman.

"It was an absolutely amazing idea for a party." I beam at him, entwining my fingers in his and then turning back to the sky. "If I wasn't already, then I would have definitely agreed to be your girlfriend after this."

"Period," we both say at the same time.

He squeezes my hand as we laugh.

"I always knew, you know?" He strokes the back of my knuckles with his thumb.

"Knew what?"

"That I wanted you to be mine forever. Even that first night together. But I couldn't say it then. You'd have run a mile."

"I might not have. I was enjoying taking turns to be in control. Who knew I'd be so good at sharing it?"

I raise an eyebrow and smile as he looks at me.

"Who knew I would, too." He smirks. "I was always going to fight for you, Shona. After Josh…" He shakes his head, shutting his eyes for a second. "After Josh, I told myself I'd wait as long as it took to get you back. It was a fight I was never going to let myself lose. You're everything I've waited for."

A calm descends around us as I move my fingers inside his, embracing his warm skin.

"I waited for you too. I didn't even realize that's what I was doing. But I needed you, Trent. I needed someone to show me what a happy relationship looks like. One with mutual respect."

"I'll always have your back, Darling. Always."

A bright glow steals my attention.

"Hey, a shooting star!" I gasp in delight as it flies across the ceiling high above us. "Make a wish, Sparky." I elbow him in the ribs.

"I don't need to. I have everything I need right here."

I turn to him, narrowing my eyes playfully. "All this romantic sweetness keeps coming from your gruff mouth. I'm not used to it."

He chuckles, and it's deep and rich, and everything I've missed this past week... maybe my entire life.

"Perhaps I should stick to the explosions and lights. I can write it in the sky instead. Tell you I love you that way."

Time freezes as our breathing halts at the exact same second.

"You love me?"

He nods, a beautiful smile taking over his face. "I do. Period."

Warmth cascades through my body.

"I love you too. Period."

"All the stars in the sky?" He quirks a brow and presses a remote. The ceiling lights up in one giant explosion of shooting stars, racing around us like we are in an alternate universe.

Somewhere magical.

And perfect.

"Show off." I laugh as he pulls me into his side.

"For you, Darling. Anything."

"Can I have one more thing for my birthday?"

"Anything." He kisses my temple.

I trail my fingers up his chest and unbutton his shirt. "I've never been naked under the night sky."

He sucks in a breath. "If you'd said, I'd have cut the power to force our guests out hours ago."

He chuckles before taking my lips with his and expertly freeing me of my dress.

I moan as his lips dust over my neck, sending tingles careering up my spine.

"Trent…"

He pulls back to look at me, his gaze darkening. "You're so beautiful. This last week, not being able to touch you… to—"

I press a finger to his lips, nodding, as unspoken words pass between us in our heated gaze.

It's been too long. We should never have been apart. Never.

"Everything from now on… it's us… you and me. Together," I whisper.

He wraps a hand around the back of my neck and pulls me to him, his lips soft and warm as our kiss turns urgent, and I push his shirt off his shoulders and undo his belt.

"It's my turn to go first this time," I say as he pushes down his pants.

"Your turn?" I wrap my hand around his rigid cock and stroke to the base.

"At giving orders." I draw my hand back and unsnap my bra with my free hand, then wriggle out of my panties.

The look on his face turns to pure lust as he races to rid himself of his pants.

"I've hated every second of this last week. Until today. I need to feel you inside me again. I need you to fill the emptiness that being apart has caused."

I pull him on top of me, spreading my legs wide around his hips.

"I know, Darling. I know... We need to make up properly."

I let out a soft laugh as he smiles at me.

"We do. I've missed your personal special effects demonstrations."

"And, Jesus, I've missed this," he hisses as he holds my gaze and pushes inside me.

Our mouths drop open in a unified moan as he fills every space inside me until my thighs tremble with the need for him to move.

"Please, Trent. Fuck me like you mean it. Erase the last seven days. I need to feel—"

He draws back, jutting his chin as he drives back in deep, causing me to cry out in pleasure and grab onto his firm ass cheeks.

"Like this?"

Thrust.

"You need to feel me?"

Thrust.

"You need me to push deep inside your cunt like it's the only place in existence I want to be."

Thrust.

"Yes, god, yes!" I cry as I spread my legs wider, welcoming the force of his movements as he thrusts into me.

"Jesus, you're so fucking wet."

His dark hair falls in his eyes, and he rakes his hand back through it with a grunt, then rises to his knees, holding my legs open.

"Put them on your shoulders."

He lets out a deep groan.

"Whatever you say, Darling. It's your turn in charge."

I smile at him as he lifts my legs over his shoulders, then leans over me so he can slide even deeper.

"Trent!" I gasp as the head of his cock rubs my G-spot and my eyes damn near roll out of my head.

"You like it deep, don't you?"

"Uh-huh, I feel so full of you," I cry, my body rippling around him as it sucks him in greedily with each thrust.

I'm still amazed it even fits in there.

Who knew all this time, Trent had the cock of dreams? It's long and thick, and since we discussed ditching condoms a couple of weeks ago, I've been coming even harder. It's like our bodies were engineered to set one another off, like one of Trent's award-winning on-set explosions.

It's the angle. The rim of his head hits me right on my—

"Fuck," I moan as pressure builds low inside my core.

Trent matches my moan with his own as he pumps into me, repeatedly, driving the tingling over my skin further and further around my body until I'm shaking with the need to come.

"Trent…"

"Come for me, Darling. Come all over my cock as I fill you," he hisses, pushing forward to kiss me before drawing back and pushing deeper inside me.

I stare at the exploding stars behind him as my orgasm breaks, splintering into a thousand pieces like the glittering lights behind him.

"Oh, fuck... Trent..."

I look into his eyes, my orgasm deepening and making my body tighten around his cock.

His pupils dilate.

"Jesus, you're..."

I clench around him more forcefully, urging him deeper.

"You're fucking unique," he growls, dropping forward again to catch my lips in an urgent kiss. "You're everything, Shona. I love you."

Then he groans, and it's there... liquid heat, like starlight, spreading inside me, bringing brightness to the dark corners of myself that I kept hidden. Shining brightly on the memories that used to plague me with their ugliness, burning the pain of them away. Trent's confessions of love spilling from his lips exposes them, bringing them out of the shadows to where they no longer seem so frightening.

To where they are no longer the most defining thing that's ever happened to me.

Not anymore.

He's blown them out of the sky, sent them ricocheting far, far away. Like they've been strapped to a rocket, and he lit the fuse.

With one beautiful spark.

Sparky.

The grumpy boss who owns my heart. Who I can no longer imagine life without.

The man who made me his.

Period.

Mr. Trent Forde.

Chapter 16
Trent

Epilogue

"Oh, Mom," I murmur as I pass the hallway table.

The frame is back out of the drawer again. I considered taking it away, or tossing the photo in the garbage, but thought it might confuse her more. She has good days and bad days. On the good ones, I've pointed out Claudia and Ewan and explained that's why the picture is in the drawer, and she understands.

But it keeps finding its way back out again.

I reach for it, halting midway.

Then I grab the frame and bring it closer to my face.

Claudia and Ewan are no longer smiling back at me with deceit. In their place is a photograph of me, Mom, and Shona, taken at Shona's birthday party a couple of weeks ago.

The night I got my brightly burning, copper-ringed star back.

I trace the cool glass and my mouth lifts into a smile. Maybe Shona did it? Or Mom? Either way, it's the best damn photograph I have in this whole house.

I place it down, positioning it so it can be seen from all angles.

"Trent?" Mom calls. "Did you order them yet?"

I chuckle as I walk into the kitchen where she is drinking a cup of tea.

"No wonder you and Shona get on so well, both always got something you want me to do."

"Stop talking, Trent. Start doing. You can't miss your chance."

"Okay, okay." I smile and pull out my cell phone with one hand, wrapping my fingers around the object in my pocket with my other hand as I dial.

"Hello, you're through to Cygnature Blooms, where bigger is always better. We specialize in healing broken hearts worldwide. May I have your location to connect you to your closest store, please?"

"LA, please, Hollywood."

"Yes, I'd like to order a bouquet of forget-me-nots, please," I say to the young woman who answers. "Can you please put, *'Shona, my Darling. Entertain my selfishness, please. Because there's no one else I would rather have challenge me for the rest of my life.'* Then can you add something to the back of the card, too?"

"Of course, sir. What would you like there?"

I stroke the soft velvet of the ring box inside my pocket.

"*'Say yes. Period.'*"

The End

Chapter 17
Elle's Books

Forget-Me-Nots & Fireworks is novella length prequel to 'The Men Series', a collection of interconnected standalone stories.
They can be read in any order, however, for full enjoyment of the overlapping characters, the suggested reading order is:

Meeting Mr. Anderson – Holly and Jay
Discovering Mr. X – Rachel and Tanner
Drawn to Mr. King – Megan and Jaxon
Captured by Mr. Wild – Daisy and Blake
Pleasing Mr. Parker – Maria and Griffin
Trapped with Mr. Walker – Harley and Reed
Time with Mr. Silver – Rose and Dax
Resisting Mr. Rich – Logan and Maddy

Get all of Elle's books here: http://author.to/ellenicoll

Chapter 18
Wild Blooms

Complete WILD BLOOMS Series

Don't forget to leave a review for your favourite books.

Snapdragons and Seductions - Sofia Aves

Saffron and Secrets - Sharon Woods

Blossom and Bliss - L.A. Shaw

Willows and Waterlilies - Taylor K Scott

Roses and Redemption - Denise T Ford

Wildflowers and Whispers - Maci Dillon

Bluebonnets and Bikers - D. Lilac

Magnolias and Memories - T M Caruso

Lavender and Lust - Jaclyn Combe

Jasmine and Jealousy - Rhiannon Marina

Tulips and Truths - Mila Chase

Lilacs and Lovers - J R Gale

Chrysanthemum and Smolder - V L Peters

Lotus and Longing - LaLa Montgomery

Daisies and Desire - Ann Penny

Sunflowers and Surrender - L M Fox

Forget-me-nots and Fireworks - Elle Nicoll

Peonies and Promises - Lizzie Moreton

Heather and Heartache - VR Tennent
All books are available in ebook and paperback.

Chapter 19
Acknowledgments

This book is part of the 'Wild Blooms' Series.
Wild Blooms began with some of the authors who have been inspired by TL Swan to chase their dreams and see where their words take them. I am so incredibly proud and blessed to be part of such an inspirational group of people.

So, thank you TL Swan and all of the Cygnets, you're all incredible.

Sara, my super organised PA, and our amazing street and ARC teams, I couldn't do this without you all. You blow me away with your support.

My beta readers; Sara, Taye, and Rita. Thank you for embracing this novella when you're used to my chunky books landing in your emails.

Zee, my editor, thank you for the SHOUTY caps, and for being wise and wonderful.

Thank you to Sarah for a beautiful cover. I'm so excited to have a couple cover for the first time. And one in colour!

Finally, thank you to you for reading Shona and Trent's story. I hope it brought some joy to your day. If you'd like to leave a review for it, then I'll be very grateful.

Thank you, and until the next book...
Elle x

Chapter 20
About Elle

Elle Nicoll is an ex long-haul flight attendant from the UK.

After fourteen years of having her head in the clouds whilst working at 38,000ft, she is now usually found with her head between the pages of a book reading or furiously typing and making notes on another new idea for a book boyfriend who is sweet-talking her. Elle finds it funny that she's frequently told she looks too sweet and innocent to write a steamy book, but she never wants to stop. Writing stories about people, passion, and love, what better thing is there?

Because,

Love Always Wins

xxx

To keep up to date with the latest news and releases, find Elle in the following places, and sign up for her newsletter below;

https://www.subscribepage.com/ellenicollauthorcom
Facebook Reader Group – Love always Wins – https://www.facebook.com/groups/686742179258218
Website – https://www.ellenicollauthor.com

Printed in Great Britain
by Amazon